A

THE FEAST OF THE WOLF

The
Feast of the Wolf

—

THOMAS BLACKBURN

MacGibbon & Kee   London

Granada Publishing Limited
First published in Great Britain 1971 by MacGibbon & Kee Ltd
3 Upper James Street London W1R 4BP

Copyright © 1971 by Thomas Blackburn

ISBN 0 261 63214 0
Printed in Great Britain by Novello & Co Ltd
Borough Green Kent

FOR MARGARET

1

Simon Armstrong, MA, PhD, DLitt, FRSL reviewed the inaugural lecture he was to give at his metropolitan university with anxiety and satisfaction. Although he had worked for ten years as Senior Lecturer at his College, he had not expected to be offered the chair of English. He was a poet and writer of some distinction but, far from being a recommendation to forty-five per cent of the Senate who had considered his appointment, such distinction was evidence of instability. 'No doubt it is,' he thought, 'God knows I'm unstable enough. I can't tell whether I will ever be illustrious—I certainly don't feel it now, but then these dons do make a fat living from dead men they'd have avoided like the plague when alive.'

Dr Emily Wragg, for instance, an Elizabethan expert and one of his principal opponents; what would have been her reaction to the Christopher Marlowe she extolled in lecture after lecture, if she had actually met that savage and bisexual genius? He would have pounced like a stoat. Well clawed, she would have been hauled off by her sycophantic Lesbians—Armstrong used that term with remarkable looseness—and revived with sweet sherry and cake.

Would Mr Henry Dodd, the 'lad with the delegate air', have enjoyed the company of the poet Rimbaud, of whom he had written a distinguished appraisal, if that terrible adolescent had actually swayed into one of his seminars and exploded his dreary monologues, to the delight of his passive victims? He would have growled with disgust at the actuality of his 'hero' and sent a report to the Proctors.

But Laura, his wife, was right about the inaugural lecture; he would give them the first chapter of the book he was now working on, *The Cult of the Vampire*, and not play safe and give them a rehash of his recent critique of Lord Tennyson. '*The Cult of the Vampire*', Simon felt a prickling of excitement and terror running along his spine. The book was very near to a personal confusion which he had by no means solved, and his wife had good cause to be frightened of. The dark side of his planet. He wished it neatly away on to the Psychology Department. They would be after him for poaching.

Let them; he'd had ten years of psychiatric treatment and suspected that a good deal of experimental psychology was a refuge from terror. They went in for curves of effect and rats because this is what attracted them to Psychology in the first place; they were scared, scared stiff of themselves. No wonder. He didn't quite know what Vampires were, but was frightened of what they made him feel—that was why he was so busy on the book. 'Authors bleed into their work,' he thought, 'it's wisdom sweated out from fear and confusion.'

Wisdom; for the most part. But there were the off-beat exceptions. Could you really enjoy Swinburne's first book without a taste for flagellation—Our Lady of Pain, Faustine? 'Not my line.'

He thought of the minute bard skipping off to spend his sixpenny allowance on a beer or two at the Green Man, being ecstatic over babies to the consternation of their nurses on Putney Heath, and he remembered a brief meeting with the aged wife of the poet's mentor.

'They were dear boys,' she had creaked, 'such dear good boys.'

'It must have been exciting living with two men like that. You must have had some remarkable experiences.'

'Dear boys,' Mrs Watts-Dunton puckered her moist, red-rimmed eyes and wandered back through the years. 'One thing was perhaps a little puzzling.'

'I would be fascinated to hear,' Simon had ferreted.

'I never really understood it but now and again they would ask me to take my clothes off and lie on the bed. Strange. They would sprinkle me with chocolate powder, *all* over, mind you, then—lick it off, giggling like a pair of schoolboys! Mind you, there was nothing wrong with it.'

'On the contrary, it must have been extremely nourishing.'

Mrs Watts-Dunton smiled her musing agreement. Anything except overt sexuality was an acceptable part of the life she had determined to make pleasant for the 'dear boys'.

What would she have made of De Sade? Simon searched for the appropriate euphemism. 'Such an excitable young man! But he really did, in his own way, love beauty.' He thought of the last days of the verbose, aristocratic madman; how he would gather roses from the asylum garden, a nice little bunch, take them to a dribble of dirty water that stemmed from the kitchen, then, flower by flower, grind them into the messy refuse.

But tomorrow the lecture. He realised how intimately *The Cult of the Vampire* was connected with his early life and again felt a tremor of excitement. Back, always backward into the half world where ghosts were reality. He remembered the journey he had made with Rosalind; she was a friend now and no longer the remote alienist and guide. They had gone through his Cretan Maze until there at the dead centre was the thing itself, stinking of pus and stale milk, no bull-headed monster but a septic nipple. He could recall the bitter taste and stringy texture of the milk, the foul dug from which, since one breast could not nourish a famished baby, he had fought for life with toothless gums.

His mother had filled in the gaps with the compulsion of those who, dying, wish to make peace with their past life.

'Nurse Erpenshore said I must wean you, darling, but I couldn't bear to do it. You see your grandmother died, left me alone when I was only six and I knew, whatever the cost, I must give you the mother's love I never had, all I could offer.'

'Dear mother!' he thought. 'As usual the road to hell'—and it had been hell—'is paved with the very best intentions.'

'Then both breasts went dry,' the flat dead voice rambled on. 'Nurse Erpenshore said, "Now you'll just have to wean him and a mercy it is." She didn't understand.'

'Go on, mother,' Simon had taken notes from the once formidable woman who was now half blind and octogenarian.

'You wouldn't take to the bottle, darling, you wanted me, me, me, but I couldn't feed you. Those were bad days, you lay there like a little ghost; and wouldn't take your bottle, you lost half your weight; you died, nearly.'

'Before that I must have hurt you.'

'You did, my pet, but I loved you so much I was able to bear it.' Simon realised again that his first experience of life was associated with the giving and taking of pain. That to suck was to give pain and destroy. That to be sucked was to suffer and find some devious pleasure in the pain of it. No wonder he was writing *The Cult of the Vampire*.

His mother was dead now and had died with rectitude, refusing opiates, working her way to death as she had worked for the birth of her children. Anyway, it was the difficulty of his nurture, the bad weaning, his mother's later fear of childish vitality and of temper tantrums, that had forced him to explore the recesses of his own mind and gain some understanding. Cheap at the price. The knowledge he had gained from that backward and under-ground journey was the source of his poetry and the half-finished book, part of which was to be the theme of his inaugural lecture. Tomorrow; again he felt the nervous tingling. 'God knows how the old busters will take it,' he wondered as he got into bed beside his wife.

He was irritated that she was already asleep, and he had undressed noisily, kicking his clothes off and knocking over a chair. She had woken up as he bounced down beside her.

'Are you cross because I fell asleep?'

'Yes,' he said kissing her, 'will you be there tomorrow?'

'Of course I will, I wouldn't miss it for anything. I've only got to see little Stephen Woodward at Wall End and that will be finished by twelve o'clock.'

After her English Degree (she had been Simon's favourite student), Laura had taken a Diploma in Psychology and now was a Psychiatric Social Worker and did part-time duties at a hospital for disturbed children.

'Good, you know how much it reassures me to have you there in the audience. We can check up afterwards.'

'We can indeed.' Laura knew only too well the endless post-mortems after her husband's lectures and readings. 'But you'll knock them cold when you get going. You always do.'

'Will I? I need you to tell me, you know.'

'You will,' Laura put her arms round her husband

nestling against her, 'and now, my darling, do let's go to sleep.'

2

'DISTINGUISHED poet—accolade of the Golden Treasury—
definitive study of Lord Tennyson's poetry—handbook of
poetry for schools . . .'

The Vice-Chancellor introduced him with a number of
well-chosen clichés which seemed to apply to a creature from
another planet. Two purple hearts warm in his stomach,
Professor Armstrong studied the geography of his audience
with Olympian detachment. Next to Laura in the front
row was Professor Emeritus Johnson Day. He had been
Simon's main support for the chair. His voice muttered
excitedly to Laura throughout the introduction. Simon
marvelled that someone with two or three remarkably
strange delusions, who had probably never kissed a woman
except his mother, who went to bed at nine o'clock with a
mug of cocoa and composed his penetrating studies of
English Literature over Horlicks, could have such a pro-
found understanding of human nature and the complexities
of Shakespeare.

Left centre was the English brigade. Dr Hicks, his senior,
and the more likely candidate for his chair, was quietly
biting his nails, while two other colleagues were exchanging
those splenetic wisecracks which are often the accompani-
ment of a high IQ and retarded feelings. Next came the
Psychologists; Dr Puttrell, round, pink and a Watsonian
Behaviourist, was at the centre of his form-fillers and key-
tappers. He had a nasty look. The Doctor bitterly resented
Simon's interweaving of psychology, myth and literature.
Everything for Puttrell must be neatly tabulated, pinned
down by labels on a sheet of white paper—dead.

'We can be sure that there never existed man-beasts like
the Minotaur, whose body was hairy and human but whose
head was that of a bull. We can be sure that for earlier
generations this terrible image best expressed their sense
of the everyday human being dominated by ferocious
animalic energy. The same applies to the werewolf, domina-

14

tion by some man-killing power of the unconscious. A great healer, Jesus Christ, expresses it in his last, best and least recognised book, the Gospel of Thomas. "Blessed is the lion that the man eats, and the lion will become a man; and cursed is the man the lion eats, and the lion will become a man".'

'Objection!' Armstrong had told the Vice-Chancellor that he was willing to be interrupted and to answer questions in the course of his lecture; as he looked at the furious foxy little face of Brother Julian, an Anglican Franciscan Friar and member of the Theological Department, but for his purple hearts he might have regretted the decision.

'Not only do I object to Professor Armstrong trespassing on the territory of professional theologians, but I resent his naïve assumption that the Gospel of Thomas with its half-baked Gnostic generalisations is connected with the teaching and ministry of Our Saviour.'

'Literature is part of life, Brother Julian, and I assume you do admit that theology has the same concern, so it is difficult to deny they are involved with similar situations. As for the Gospel of Thomas, I am not concerned with definitive statements, faith or scholastic proof as to its authenticity; only the elucidation of some human problems. For me the book is a most penetrating exploration of some human problems.'

Brother Julian sat down muttering, but there was a growl from the ranks of the behaviourists—they were steaming up.

'One is aware that repressed and, in consequence, dangerous energies can separate themselves off from human psyche and then, returning like thieves in the night, dominate the men and women who, since unconscious really does mean unconscious, have no idea of their existence. But what if these repressed energies should be reinforced by similar destructive forces looking for a host, having no local habitation and existing in that twilight area which Jung called the Collective Unconscious and Tibetan Buddhists the Bardo—a half world of potent shades. If that be the case, then may I suggest that Christ's "possession by devils" is more relevant than other terms to this state of malevolent control and withdrawal?'

'No, you certainly may not!'

It was Dr Puttrell who, in his desire to prove that human beings are the automata of their glands, had inflicted great pain on innumerable white rats. He was very flushed and Simon looked at him with speculative interest. Not for the first time Laura remarked the difference between her husband on the platform, bland, impeccable, intelligent and mature, with the petulant beer-swilling child she had often had to deal with after a lecture—his great need of reassurance and affection.

Puttrell boomed through the hall, 'What you are trying to do, young man, is bring back all the old mumbo-jumbo of bogus religiosity. Just the kind of old wives' tales that serious psychologists have been trying to sweat out of the human system for the last fifty years. But human beings are not ghosts or zombies.'

'Neither are they white rats!'

'Hear, hear,' fluted Professor Johnson Day, scenting a conflict between spirit and matter.

'I agree that we are deeply influenced in our behaviour by glandular secretions, that there is a chemical basis to human nature, that much of our behaviour is dependent on reflexes, but that is only a part of the story.'

'Its the only part that can be taken seriously by serious scientists,' Puttrell flushed even more deeply. 'You, you are regressing, to use your own words, to a form of faith healing and witchcraft that can do nothing but harm. You are a sensationalist, you have no case to prove.'

Simon winked at Laura. 'A sensationalist I may be, but I have no case to prove, only a few tentative observations to make. Anyway, even you, Dr Puttrell, must have heard of the work of Dr Karl Jung.'

'Another charlatan,' bellowed Puttrell, 'a mystagogue!'

'Thank you, Dr Puttrell, for your most interesting contribution. But I would imagine that most people here agree with me that Dr Jung has made a not unimportant contribution to psychiatry and are familiar with his theory of archetypes. Now, most archetypes must have some counterpart in the physical world, the wise old woman, the seer, the Wandering Jew, the eagle, the serpent, the phoenix.

But we have in the Vampire an image which seems to have occurred in Europe some time before anything was known of its physical counterpart in South America, the bat which not only sucks the blood of other creatures, which is parasitic upon the blood of others but—this is indeed remarkable—if it feeds on its relation, the harmless fruit-bat, can change that creature into another vampire. We have an archetype which occurred in Europe before we were familiar with its physical counterpart . . .'

Laura smiled reassuringly at Simon as Dr Puttrell rose to propose his vote of thanks. It was not a happy choice but the Vice-Chancellor was not noted for his tact.

'It is Yule Tide; who, at such a carefree, if sociologically speaking highly dubious season, can fail to have enjoyed Professor Armstrong's charming fairy stories, garnished as they were by so many pretty touches of literary fantasy?'

As soon as the lecture was over, Simon moved down to his wife.

'Was I alright darling, did it come over?'

'Perfect, absolutely clear, they were all fascinated.'

'But Puttrell?'

'Oh never mind him, what did you expect? You were fine.'

But despite Laura and Johnson Day's congratulations, Simon was fuming sulkily when they got home, and Laura had a bad time restoring his ruffled ego.

'If ever there was a bloody vampire, it's that old swine,' he muttered, 'I bet he sleeps on good Kentish soil and uses a bag of live rats as a hotwater bottle.'

Consoled by his wife, he finally rumbled off to sleep. Birds were twittering, no, not birds, those thin flute noises and cries that wove through the fat fleshy leaves. He went more deeply into his dream. 'This,' he thought, 'has nothing to do with what I personally know; the Backs at Cambridge, for instance, with their tutored vegetation, the cool ethics of an Alpine pinewood. Here you live or die depending on whether you can suck the sap of another tree, or working through gross foliage reach some gasp of sky and sunlight.' Then the face came, sliding to his passive body down a blurred shaft of sunlight. At first it was merely a faint oval, then he saw the grey mottled skin of its features and a thatch of reddish hair. Its body a mere following shadow, its scaled wings palpitating, it glided towards him, bestial but with a suggestion of humanity. Its small pointed ears were tufted with sharp hair, its nose was flattened leaflike against its face, the nostrils black holes, so that the long curved lips and teeth protruded beyond them. It had no chin but its mouth was held up by twitching tendons. He could not move and he could smell its breath, the sweet sour odour of tainted meat.

'You hunger, you thirst.'

The words shaped themselves in his brain and Simon experienced to the last intolerable farthing that extremity of thirst, hunger and suffocation which he had known struggling for milk as an unweaned child.

'Believe me, and you will hunger and thirst no more. I will give you not living water but the blood of life itself. You will drink my blood, I will drink of your blood and in this communion—which shall last world without end, you will be at peace.'

He felt rough hairs brushing his forehead. Small clawed fingers were fumbling at his pyjama buttons and the fanged lips bent down to his throat. Then the light started. Behind the creature cool, serene and increasing in intensity, it glowed down and forward until as in an X-ray photograph, the light seemed to penetrate the texture of the muzzle that was bending over him, and disintegrate it until he could see no bones or muscle, only a pink mist. For a moment the light held the ghost of the creature's features in a convulsion of fear and loathing, then it vapoured into nothing. But the light seemed to condense and he was looking into a girl's face of extreme sweetness. They said nothing but there was an infinite depth of meeting and comprehension. He could find no words but when he woke up and remembered his dream, he knew that whatever happened—and indeed it would happen and it would be terrible, since the face and the light existed—'Thou hast delivered my soul from Hell, my darling from the power of the dog'—the conclusion could never be other than satisfactory.

'Do turn over,' said Laura, 'you've been grinding your teeth and muttering.'

'I can well believe it,' he said, 'but—Rhoda—I am quite clear now, we must have her.'

'Thank God for that,' thought Laura. She had long chafed at a childless marriage and it was perhaps this accepted frustration that had accentuated the bronchial tendency she had developed over the years. Now there sounded real conviction in her husband's voice. The adoption would take place and she felt sure it would bring as much happiness to Simon as to herself, as well as the little girl who had been offered to them. It seemed a step in the fulfillment of the destiny in which she believed with fervour. The excitement caused her to cough nervously but she stifled the noise in the pillow and went to sleep.

3

SIMON AND LAURA were settled in a corner of The Rover before a do at the Vice-Chancellor's. He looked at her affectionately over his glass of beer.

'I did like that water colour you painted today—of the almond blossom.'

'Yes, so do I, it's accurate, it's got what I wanted.'

'I could see you from my study. You just sat absolutely still watching the tree for almost an hour, then started and in about five minutes the thing was finished.'

'Yes, I wait till the image sort of congeals in my mind. Then when it's ready I just put it down. In water colours, you must keep it fluid so you must be quick.'

'Why don't you let me arrange an exhibition in the Senate House?'

Laura looked worried and started to cough. 'Time enough for that,' she gasped. 'The point is to get more pictures done. I like painting only for my own pleasure. Give me a cigarette.'

'Ought you to? You're coughing, you know.'

'And I'm going to enjoy the party. Come on, hand one over.'

'Here you are, but darling, why didn't you wear your fur coat when you were painting? There was an east wind and you only had a jersey.'

'Two jerseys. Anyway what's a cold, I can always check the bronchitis with those pills Dr Jones gave me.'

'I wish you weren't so careless about yourself.'

'One hypochrondriac is enough in any family. Come on. Time to go.'

The Armstrongs finished their glasses of beer, Simon remarking as usual that the only good time of a party was the two or three drinks before the thing started.

It had started. When they entered the Vice-Chancellor's house where they were to absorb sherry and tittle-tattle, the place was roaring like an animal. 'Why,' Laura murmured to her husband, as they were waiting to be announced, 'do the English middle classes imagine that the absorption of indifferent sherry from six till nine p.m. is a harmless recreation?' Simon slapped his pocket sagely—there was a quarter of a bottle of gin in it. 'Watch out for the booze, Laura, Lady N buys it from her grocer in bulk at a handsome discount.'

'Professor and Mrs Simon Armstrong.'

The usher's words were swallowed up by the racket, but there was the Vice-Chancellor looking as usual damp and diminished beside his strapping wife. Lady Nevis was an angular buck-toothed opinionated woman. Desire to avoid her company had played no small part in Sir John's career.

'John! Stop day-dreaming, it's the Armstrongs.' He smiled wanly, then winced as his wife's bony elbow rammed home.

Nevis was trapped for the moment, but was off to a conference the next day. Indeed he had scurried for two decades from conference to conference and from committee to committee, spurred by those winged words with which his wife could deflate his all too vulnerable self-esteem. The result had been the Vice-Chancellorship of a distinguished university and a knighthood. But there was no bolthole that evening.

Lady Nevis fixed Simon with a ferocious eye. 'And what, Professor Armstrong, do you think of your colleague's latest book? Quite definitive as far as I'm concerned.'

'Quite, quite definitive, Lady Nevis.'

He was aware of Laura rolling her eyes heavenward—in this book there was little of Johnson Day's genius, but a great deal of the off-beat side of his personality. They had marvelled that he could air it in print. But Simon had no desire to do battle.

'So true to life,' Lady Nevis boomed.

'Perversion is the power house of all great art,' Laura quoted the Professor's opening gambit.

'Precisely; the fairest flowers grow from the grossest mud, even the greatest men have their little foibles.' She gave a side-kick of a glance at her husband who was talking happily to a fellow educationalist.

'Ah, the strangeness of life,' murmured Laura remembering that except for a couple of false premises and a complete falsification of Shelley's known life history, Johnson had produced a deft study of the poet as an androgynous pervert who abhorred any natural connection between a man and a woman.

'Not even a cockroach would be safe when the bard was in his moods,' said Simon.

Lady Nevis was a little deaf and neighed with pleasure, her flared nostrils distended. 'How right you are, dear Professor, that book will certainly annoy the prudes!'

Glassy-eyed, the Reverend Professor Stagpoole weaved towards them, holding a tumbler of brown liquid in one hand and a sodden cigar in the other. His small, ferrety wife skipped behind him with an ashtray, vainly trying to protect the Vice-Chancellor's carpet from her husband's trail of cigar ash. The Head of the Theology Department was both erudite and bibulous.

'Congratulations, my dear boy, and to you, dear Laura. We have a West Indian in charge of the Biology Department, a Freemason in the French, and now a poet as Professor of English, truly my cup runneth over.' He slopped sherry onto the carpet. 'You know, my dear boy, I am a devotee of your verse.' Stagpoole was quite indifferent to his wife who was on her knees mopping up the sherry with some of the paper handkerchiefs she kept for such occasions. 'It contains so many interesting heresies. In Victorian England, when Sir James Stephen was appointed Regius Professor of Modern English at Cambridge, Dr Corrie, the Master of Jesus College, nodded to Archdeacon Hardwick, and observed, "Who would have thought we should have seen a live Gnostic walking about the streets of Cambridge? You know, my friend, in healthier times he would have been burnt." Lucky you weren't born in the Middle Ages or you'd have been for the stake. Well, carry on with the good work, my dear boy.'

He glanced down at Mrs Stagpoole, 'I am neglecting my good wife, come, my love, and I will see that your glass is replenished.' He rolled majestically towards the buffet, Mrs Stagpoole snapping vainly at his heels.

'How on earth do they ever manage to get married?' asked

Laura.

'They're so busy reading books that they don't realise what's happened until it's too late. Their mothers arrange it.' He pictured the expression of some earnest pedant when he rolled over in bed and found a strange becurlered head sharing his pillow. 'Mind you, Mums don't always further marriage, look at John Hicks making his entrance with that American postgraduate from Princeton.'

Blushing deep red, Hicks, an eighteenth-century expert, was introducing his most recent acquaintance to Sir Charles and Lady Nevis with a guilty furtiveness more appropriate to a curate entering a brothel.

'He shifts from foot to foot, he's a nice hue of scarlet. No doubt Mum's waiting at home for her wandering boy. I bet he's impotent as a china tom.'

'How nicely you put it "Professor Armstrong,",', said Laura.

'Whack-oh, me lucky lad! and how are all the little imps and impesses, not to mention Count Dracula himself, this bitter evening?' A flabby hand descended on Simon's shoulder.

'Darling!' Laura gasped, for her husband had spun round and shot a hard-fisted thumb into the soft belly of Professor Puttrell.

The Watsonian sank slowly to the floor and in the immediate neighbourhood there was a sudden silence; Puttrell was not noted for his heavy drinking.

'My dear Dr Puttrell!' Shocked at his own violent reaction, Simon helped Puttrell to his feet and dusted him down. 'My most sincere apologies! Reflexes, entirely reflexes.'

'To hell with reflexes, you have assaulted me, sir, you are in a state of chaos, you have assaulted me, you have ...'

'Sorry to butt in,' it was one of Armstrong's rock-climbing friends John Craxton, a lecturer on Criminal Law, 'but as far as the law goes, it was you who committed the assault, a violent blow between the shoulder-blades, my dear Dr Puttrell! What with that and provocative statements to which I can bear witness, you haven't a legal leg to stand on, old man!'

Puttrell's face changed from white to purple.

'You hit me, sir, you hit me in the stomach, you may have caused grievous bodily harm.'

'And how are your shoulders, Professor Armstrong, slipped a disc, perhaps? That was the first offence, and I noted your need for self-protection.' The lawyer gave a very sharp look at the deflated Puttrell.

'It's nothing,' said Laura, 'I'm so sorry, but my husband —his war training! Your, if I may say so, aggressive stimulus set off an aggressive response.'

Puttrell looked mollified and nodded.

'I had to defend a postman recently,' said the lawyer. 'He killed a dog that went for him on his rounds. The chap was an ex-Commando trained to defend himself against the guard dogs of German prison camps. It was quite automatic for him. The dog leaps at the throat, the soldier by exact training grasps the front legs of the beast and it's torn apart by the force of its leap. Not that Armstrong is a Commando postman, Dr Puttrell, or you an alsatian. But in both cases, it's a conditioned response to aggression.'

'Automatic,' said Simon, 'you see how this little incident bears out your theory of conditioned reflexes.'

'Automatic,' Puttrell relished the word, 'Well, if I've made a convert it's worth a little physical discomfort, but you have a remarkably hard fist, young man,' he stroked his massive stomach.

'And the experiments,' said Laura, both shocked and pleased by the dexterity of her husband and his friend, 'I trust they prosper.'

Professor Puttrell had no chance to answer.

'Let's make a Welsh climbing weekend soon,' said the criminologist as another professional loomed towards them.

'Well my dear, dear friends, and have we come to our so important little decision?' The Reverend Dr Cowling was not only University Chaplain, but rich and reputed by the more scandal-mongering undergraduates to sleep with the sister who kept house for him, in a sixteenth-century four-poster, under a Gothic crucifix.

'Yes Father James,' Simon put an arm affectionately round Laura. 'My wife and I are quite sure now. We would love to have the child and may I say how grateful we are for your devoted efforts.'

Cowling was a modernist. From over the soft turtle-neck jersey which served him for a dog-collar, he beamed at his two new customers.

'I could not be happier; such a wonderful home for such a darling child. Umph, umph,' he kissed his small mani-cured hand at Simon and Laura. 'A little beige perhaps, unlike my jumper, a little "off-white"—oh, these commer-cials!—but that's the way it is and thank "You know who", you have no stupid prejudices. That's the way it is nowa-days—

> Naughty girls who jump the gun
> Choose black boys for their bit of fun.'

Not for the first time Laura was astounded at the Chap-lain's humour. 'The man,' she surmised, 'is completely amoral! Well, perhaps, that's what it means to be a Christian.'

Cowling nudged Professor Armstrong, 'You dons, if I may say so, are not only a remarkable infertile lot, but prejudiced too. In the old days, before immigration, our lasses used to turn out an average of ten pure-white bastards per annum, and how you fellows scrambled for them! Ah well, "God moves in a mysterious way, His wonders to perform." It's miscegenation or nothing now; but what bigoted old things you are! I've doubled my illegitimacy rate, but a touch of the old tar brush and I'm out of business. They'll soon have to realise it's off-white or noth-ing. Anyway, you're not like that. When will you pick up little Rhoda, three o'clock at the home?'

The Armstrongs nodded and the Reverend Cowling steered off to further converts.

'Anyone you want to meet here, or shall we make tracks for home? I fancy a quiet pint or two after all this racket.'

Laura thought for a moment. 'I wonder if Charles is here? I should love to meet him.'

Dr Abbott's appointment as head of the Psychiatry Department of the Medical School had been made despite as determined an opposition as that to Armstrong's. A

25

specialist in schizophrenia who insisted on treating his patients as human beings and their fantasies as serious contributions to science, this tall, lank, limping Cornishman was also an experimenter in LSD, and had written what had been generally described as an outrageous book about his various trips.

Certainly his inaugural lecture had been an occasion.

'There are problem students, but there are problem dons and the twain must meet,' he announced to disapproving faces who believed that they had, by the acquisition of a Doctorate, achieved near beatitude.

'If you have difficulties with your students, it is because you have difficulties within yourselves. I quote from a not unknown healer, "First cast out the beam in your own eye —it is a 'plank' in the ghastly new translation—then you will be able to see more clearly the mote in your brother's eye." We cannot see—no, that is not the right word,— understand our students until we have put our own houses in order.'

The order in Dr Abbott's 'house' that evening had not been helped by two large, noisy schizophrenics whom he had brought along for therapeutic purposes that were all his own. They had paraded like detectives along the aisles, peering into nervous faces and making comments that were both loud and caustic. They had also bawled contradictions at the quite unruffled doctor and, when they took time off from their patrol, cheered any remark that they found sympathetic.

'We are in luck,' said Laura, as they passed into a quieter room, for there by himself, gazing distastefully at his glass of sherry, was their friend Charles Abbott.

He limped forward. 'Simon and Laura, I have been meaning to ring you.'

He looked at Simon searchingly from his deep-set grey eyes. 'How much—despite his imagination and intelligence —does the fellow really know about just why the Vampire is so significant to him? The obsession is there all right but has he the strength to use it creatively? Well, there's no doubting the man's gifts, and where there's a gift there's insight.'

Abbott had been exceedingly fond of Laura when they were at the university together and though he soon realised marriage and domesticity were not for him, still took a deep interest in her and her husband.

'But it's not up to me,' he thought, 'I'm not his psychiatrist!'

He stubbed out his cigar butt with muscular fingers. 'That paper of yours, The Cult of the Vampire; we must talk. I found it of great interest. How about The Bull?'

'Excellent,' said Simon and Laura.

With a dexterous twist Abbott swished his glass of sherry into a bedraggled rubber plant and, bowing to an even more bedraggled Vice-Chancellor, followed his friends into the evening. Simon quietly insisted Laura put on the coat she had draped over a shoulder, for there was a chill frosty mist seeping up from the river. Years ago Abbott had had a bad fall while climbing the Aiguille du Midi with Armstrong; the cold brought out the pain and accentuated the limp in his left leg. But his mind was on vampires and he scarcely felt the needling ache from what remained of an impacted fracture.

4

DR ABBOTT had no small talk. Once the drinks arrived and they were settled in a corner of the saloon, he drank deeply from his pint mug, lit a cigar and started.

'We know each other's books... Always one tries to deepen and elaborate similar themes. But there were some points in your lecture I found fascinating.'

He looked expectantly at his pint mug and Simon got another round.

'We're selfish brutes. When I say "of the greatest interest" I mean we are working on the same lines and have reached somewhat similar conclusions. One has to use such terms, but like you I've always suspected emotional disassociation, repression of violence, the domination of the ego by some unconscious fantasy. Then there's old grandmother "Id" with her ragbag of all the tendencies we're not sure about. They make a pretty hollow booming sound when applied to a psychosis.'

'You prefer the terms of the Gospels,' Laura stared at him. 'Possession by devils, for instance?'

'At least it's gathered power through time. Oh, we need our psychiatric jargon, but the trouble is it may only touch the edge of the mind and miss out the heart.'

'It can remain a matter of labels,' said Simon, 'sometimes a mere form of exorcism; name the beast and, bang, it's finished. One can stop at the label and miss what lies behind.'

Abbott raised his eyes heavenward in mock sorrow. 'Certainly most of the chaps at my lecture missed the whole point. Though really I shouldn't have brought my two schitzes along, they didn't help, God bless them. But what do these chaps use their bloated brains for? Simply to arrange, in neat little patterns, powers which would frighten the daylights out of them if they got a glimpse of what they're gassing about.'

'Even psychiatrists are pretty crude,' said Simon, looking

soulfully at his half-empty pint mug, 'not to mention the behaviourists and butcher's cleaver merchants. It's all down in black and white and to hell with whether it works or not. Compulsive alcoholism, catatonic withdrawal, then a lobotomy, shock and hey-presto—you turn an interesting madman into a vegetable.'

'Exactly,' agreed Charles Abbott, 'hang on a moment while I set us up.'

He whisked neatly through the bar-barrage and returned bearing two pints and a martini in one well practised hand.

'You mentioned the vampire complex. That's a good name for it, though I noticed some pretty sour looks among my band of hope. God knows how they manage to stomach Oedipus. But the clinical stuff, I'm with you there too, breast fixation, a rather unholy stoppage at the sucking and biting stage, a failure to go on to the genital, Dracula's horror of light, and a daytime session on a bit of his mother earth, i.e. fixation on Mum. But here's the point that interests me, we've been following up the same line of thought—what if, given the clinical background, given a certain quality of repression, what if the repressed energy could be reinforced by a real vampire?'

'That's the point,' said Laura echoing Abbott's lecture-room monologue, 'some power like Dracula from no particular person, time or place entering into a shuttered-off, a repressed part of the self.'

'Yes,' Simon mused, 'what if a . . . a personal disposition attracted an energy towards itself, an energy which is impersonal, and—to use a word which would make old Puttrell shudder, "satanic"? That would shake some of your colleagues.'

'It certainly would; the disturbed mind as an attractive centre for stronger but similarly disposed energies. And why stop at one "devil"? No wonder some patients are impossible to cure—what did one of Christ's more difficult cases say? "My name is legion for we are many".'

'Many,' said Laura sipping her martini, 'and their host dwelt among the tombs and could break the chains they bound him with. Imagine all this, this "togetherness" with a single intention. Think of an obsession which corresponds with but is stronger than that of one patient. What about it then?'

'Then,' said Charles, 'you would have diabolical possession. I tell you this because one of my patients showed all the signs of becoming a vampire!'

Simon and Laura leant forward with that prickling of the skull which prefaces a new revelation and Abbott noticed with pleasure how eagerly they listened. Most of his Department would at this point have said 'goodbye' politely, and he needed to talk.

'The name is Stella Johnson.'

'Swift's girl friend,' murmured Laura, 'he certainly sucked her dry enough. The terrible cold regimen he imposed on that woman.'

Abbott nodded appreciatively.

'You're right about the Dean's Stella, but this one is not in a decline at the moment—quite the opposite. She'd got into the hands of that old buster who thinks he can cure the mind with a carving knife. You know, the lobotomy merchant, Power.'

'Power,' said Simon shuddering slightly. 'I certainly do know him.' He had narrowly missed shock and a course of Chinese brain-washing at his hands. Power, through a lengthy analysis, had come very near the centre of an intolerable psychosis and withdrawn in the nick of time. He was determined that neither he nor his patients would ever risk the road to such an infernal vision.

Abbott smiled and tapped his knee. 'Sensible people, Stella's parents. Roman Catholics often have a lot of psychological insight. They are used to Symbols. They didn't want a potato for a daughter and since Power couldn't get her certified she filtered down to me.'

'He must have been furious.'

'He certainly was; we are, as it were, at opposite ends of the psychiatric spectrum. But . . . Stella, twenty-three, a very beautiful girl. She had a disastrous foetal development, though; God knows, some nitwits insist on thinking of the womb as an impregnable Garden of Eden. Rubbish! The unborn child must be influenced by the mental and physical state of its mother. It was in St Kitts. Anything wrong?'

Both Laura and Simon started talking together. 'It's just that we happen to be adopting a child from St Kitts, or rather her mother comes from the place.'

'Nothing follows, but where are you getting her from?'

'Schwartz's home, Haydon Lodge, about three tomorrow.'

'Should be OK. I know Schwartz and I'll come round and have a look at the child. I'm interested in the island, it's by no means healthy. Take Stella's mother; they thought she had contracted rabies when she was six months gone. Luckily it was only blood poisoning, and they got the infection under control quickly enough, but I'm certain it affected Stella's development; they're the very devil, these foetal infections.'

'Now I see what you're after. I presume Stella's mother was infected by a vampire bat?'

'Filthy little beasts. Thank God it wasn't rabies, only blood poisoning, but you know they can be rabies-carriers without catching it.'

'Yes, I know that,' said Laura, 'but tell me how long was the disease latent in the mother before the symptoms appeared?'

'Only a few days, then another week before it was cleared up. Stella was probably exposed for about a fortnight. A lot can happen in a fortnight of pregnancy.'

'Just hang on a minute while I slip round the corner.'

When Simon had gone, Charles looked at Laura and his dark leathery face twisted into a smile.

'The adoption's coming off then? That will please you, and I must say I'm delighted.'

'About time too; much as I love Simon, I was getting damn fed up about his childhood—not to mention childish-obsessions. As you know it hasn't been easy.'

Abbott nodded. 'What was it?' he thought, 'an abortion? There have been rumours about it.'

He grinned lovingly into his old friend's delicate eager face. He had known her many years now and worked with her at Wall End hospital. 'Tell me about it while the gent's relieving himself. You had a hell of a time about children at the start of your marriage. What happened?'

31

Laura's eyes narrowed with remembered pain. 'He thought a child would interfere with his poetry. He more or less forced me to get rid of it. I wouldn't have let it happen now, but I was young and his tantrums really terrified me.'

'I bet they did; these mother-fixated men can be the end—they want a cross between a private milkbar and a scratching post.'

'He's changed since then, tremendously, or I couldn't have stood it. That Dr Rosalind, his psychiatrist, really did something.'

'She couldn't have done if he hadn't wanted to change. Mind you, he still thinks he needs a little extra refreshment.'

Laura looked up and saw that her husband was enjoying a meditative gin, double by the look of it, while ordering drinks in a surreptitious corner of the bar.

'That's an old trick. Then we both wanted a child, but it didn't happen, not after my . . . miscarriage.'

'That must have made you pretty bitter.'

Laura's mouth hardened as she glanced at her husband enjoying his private gin.

'It did; but as I said, he changed, and he can be greatly loving. We do need each other. Simon doesn't show it in public but he does love me.'

'And now he does want this girl. On the surface anyway. Still you may have to look out for ructions when he isn't the only pebble on the beach.'

'No doubt, but he really seems to want her, and I'm very happy about it. I wonder what made him change his mind?'

Simon rejoined them, carrying three more beers.

'Enjoy your gin?'

'Oh that!' Simon hedged a trifle guiltily. 'I want to be fresh for your tale. You were on to Stella's prenatal trauma. What was the result?'

'That's still the mysterious X factor. But can you believe this; although it was on the records they sent from St Kitts, Dr Power and his clowns never passed this bit of news on to me. It wasn't clinically relevant.'

Abbott snorted. He was a brilliant clinical psychiatrist but his pioneer work had brought much prejudice and left him lonely if unembittered.

'Oh, it was all according to the book, but I only got this bit of "irrelevant information" from the mother. Sensible woman, Mrs Johnson.'

Laura bent forward. 'Were there other factors besides the pregnancy?'

'Yes, but they . . . go along with it. Mrs J dried up after six days, a by-product of the sepsis.'

'It seems they do have psychiatrists in Trinidad, at least damn good GPs. Stella's man supplied a first-rate case history.'

Knowing he was to hear part of his own, Simon inhaled his cigarette deeply, and was glad of the gin warm in his stomach.

'A lot of it was according to the book. She found it difficult to take the bottle, lost weight, went into a coma and then got on to her feed again. Funny how they'll suddenly come round to it. Of course things were pretty rocky after that; there were obsessions, fixations; I'll come back to some of them. But the upshot was that Stella is a very tough, intelligent girl and when the family came over here she got a first-rate English degree at her university.'

'Alcoholism?' queried Simon.

'Trust you to ask that,' said Abbott, 'you've known your alcoholism.'

'On the ball, aren't we?' said Armstrong sourly.

'Nonsense, I do know something about you, Simon. You're right, of course; she did start to drink when she clocked in at the university. Not just swigging like us soaks but like your first sick ones, real back-to-the-womb, knock-out solitary bouts in her digs. That's what got her to Power. The booze is under control now, though I had to borrow a few little numbers from the pill merchants. No, there's something I haven't got down to. The GP talks about a loss of identity. You'd expect a pretty shaky ego in a girl with her background. But these blackouts went a bit further than that and started a damn sight too early. About six. She used to get out of bed at night and drift about the garden. They'd find her under the trees just standing there, moving her lips but making no sound.

What's more when they found her she didn't know who she was. "Stella darling," Mrs Johnson would say, "come along to bed, you've been sleep-walking." Now I believe the woman, believe her husband too, they're not the type to spin fantasies. "Who's Stella?" she'd ask, "I know who you are, but who is Stella?" '

'That doesn't sound case-book stuff,' said Laura, 'I've got a patient on my hands at the moment who's recovering from a black-out. Surely if it was conventional amnesia she would not only be unaware of who she was but her parents as well?'

'Precisely. They were too bright to lock her up or tie her down though I wouldn't put that past some of the beauties I know. She was never left to sleep alone, and the night-walkings stopped. Something else started. The Js were positive about this. You'd expect youngsters full of bottled-up oral aggression to grind their teeth . . .'

'He still does,' said Laura, smiling at her husband.

'All right,' Simon muttered, 'don't rub it in.'

'You bet,' Abbott grinned, 'but Stella didn't stop at grinding or even growling, she twittered.'

Laura started, 'I see what you're driving at.'

'This is a time when even I have to be strict and official. She would wake up with a little thin scream and on several occasions when her mother or father took her in their arms to reassure her, she nuzzled into their necks and—bit them. Not just a playful bite, I've seen the scar on Mrs Johnson's throat, it could have been made by an animal.'

Charles bent his head and looked really worried. 'Listen,' he said, 'I'm coming to see your future daughter. Will you come round and see Stella?'

'Of course we will,' said Simon eagerly, 'her case—excuse the word, it's too disturbing for that—is fascinating.'

Abbott looked relieved as he drained his final pint. 'I'm really delighted you will. You see, during this last week there's been another development and I've checked up on it. From time to time she can't see her face in a mirror.'

The next day when her husband had gone to work the telephone rang. It was Abbott.

'Laura love, can you manage a quick drink with me at The Bull? It's eleven fifty now, say twelve o'clock. I've a patient at one.'

'All right, Charles, but you sound anxious, what's biting you?'

'Tell you when I see you, nothing like a phone for misunderstanding, twelve then.'

Abbott looked distinctly uneasy, almost guilty when she smiled at him over a dry sherry.

'I think I'm right, I know I'm right in introducing you both to this patient of mine.'

'You don't sound at all sure. Are you frightened that Simon might start one of his crushes? It's an occupational disease of poets but as far as I know he's got over it. There hasn't been anyone for years and he has enough fans and fan-mail.'

'Then it will be all right if you both meet her. She's so nearly got over her difficulties. The devils have gone out of her, but there's a vacuum and she's somehow attracted back to disease. She's started going to a foul little night-club. I can't provide the sort of company that will suit, but you know so many writers and so on. It might do the trick; goodness knows I'm too busy to help her socially, not to mention the transference which she hasn't got out of yet.'

'You mean Simon and I could help with people? Of course we will.'

'It's not only that; this is why I wanted to meet you; with reservations; you do believe in vampires?'

'As a mental state, but they can be exorcised. I think I was almost married to one. There's no knowing what Simon could have been without his gift—a creature of the half-world.'

'We both know that, and we're both very fond of him. But here are these two people with similar backgrounds coming together because of me. Laura, am I right?'

'I've got such confidence now, I can only think how Simon could help.'

'Even with your new daughter around?'

'Why not? You know how he copes with his difficult students, brings them to the house, breaks down those awful barriers. I think of many of them whose life would have gone really badly without his help.'

'Yes, he certainly understands chaos, the off-beats; that's why I want him to meet Stella. But what if she's stronger than he is?'

'Don't you know how tough he can be? Particularly where his work's concerned, and he's working hard at the moment.'

Abbott bent forward and touched her hand. 'You've reassured me, love. Anyway, I really do believe that after a certain age, and if we have reached a certain development, and go on developing, nothing can really harm us.'

'Then what are we worrying about?' said Laura. 'Bring on your Stella and we'll see what we can do for her.'

5

DR ABBOTT had once imagined that deep thought and motor driving were compatible. He had for a time been deprived of his licence by a terrified constabulary. He was ready for the Armstrongs at two thirty and climbed gaily into the rear seat, scattering cigar ash.

'This girl of yours, what did you say she's called?'

'Rhoda,' Laura replied, 'and I'd better tell you about her.'

'You said last night that she came from the West Indies.'

'Her mother and her grandparents did; she was born at the University.'

'Parents well off?'

'Certainly, the father's a QC, I believe; a broadminded one, I don't think he was unduly worried by the presence of his daughter's bastard.'

'Then why the hell didn't his daughter look after her brat?'

Laura winced at Abbott's terms, but she went on blithely, 'You'd understand if you met Winny Gordon. She's clever and doing research for a post-graduate course, but maternal! I don't think she's got a scrap of the instinct. I gather that when Rhoda was about six months old there was a family conference and they decided to send her off to Dr Schwartz's place pending a satisfactory adoption.'

Abbott smiled. 'Now there's a man who has some idea what makes us tick. I've sent a number of really disturbed kids to him and he's worked wonders. Obviously, I don't go the whole way with him; some of that crowd's ideas are plain dotty!'

'Like planting seed according to the moon.'

'That among other fads, but he's far more on my wavelength than sixty per cent of my profession. You know his line; every human being, even if deformed, defective or mad, has an immortal soul; its the instrument that's wrong, not the player.'

'Did you hear him the other night on television?'

'Telly!' Abbott grunted.

'Quite so,' said Simon, 'I know you're bristling with prejudices. But he made a first-rate analogy. A piano and its performer. With the defective the piano is, one way or another, a pretty poor instrument, but the performer is... effective. It's our task to try and understand what the player is trying to do with his poor instrument and help him along with it.'

'Yes,' said Abbott, 'that goes with his Karma stuff. You know—a soul is born as a mongol or a defective because it is that particular physical form that best enables it to fulfil its spiritual destiny. Can't bear the word "spiritual", but I must say the theory makes sense to me. Far more to the point than being popped brand new into life like a conjurer's rabbit.'

'What was it Wordsworth said about idiots—"their lives are hidden with God".'

'That last, Simon, is another word that's had the shine rubbed off it, but I'm with the poet. A hell of a lot is hidden in the case of some of Schwartz's little monsters, but it's a marvel how much he does manage to bring into daylight.'

'His mongols, for instance,' said Laura. 'We are too much mind,' he said, 'too much intellect, with our feelings half atrophied. But the mongol is all feeling and no mind. He's here both for his own sake and to remind us how much we have lost.'

'Looks as if we're here,' said Dr Abbott, as they turned into the drive of Haydon Lodge to the sound of a percussion band. He looked approvingly at the solid Georgian house, the airy dormitories painted in white and blue, the lawns with their "Jungle Jims" and slides and swings, the glass fronted workshops.

'Dear Laura, Simon,' Dr Schwartz glowed serenely, 'you have decided to cherish Rhoda, and you have brought with you our good friend Charles.'

Abbott and Schwartz pumped hands.

'Charles, like myself,' said Schwartz, looking at the Armstrongs, 'is not particularly popular with the professionals and the text book merchants but he is one of the few curers of souls who do not attack the soul with a blow lamp and a box spanner. Perhaps he not only has the Christian name but is a Christian.'

'Coming from you, Luke, that last's a dubious compliment. But what's this about your wanting a prescription for the boy I sent you?'

'The little Jackson? You see, Simon, in England I am not a qualified doctor; am I not right to get the best of both worlds and get drugs from our good doctor? There is a ghost in the machine and that is what most matters, but the machine, it may need a little assistance. The Jackson, he has been so badly battered, for months we might wait before one word he will say to us—but with your pills? Well, one life here is short and if your pills can help him to feel and talk again a little quicker, that is good.'

Abbot handed over a phial of capsules. 'Here you are, my absent-minded seer. Twice a day only, and don't you let the little Jackson have the bottle or you'll have a ghost on your hands with no machine in it.'

'Poor child,' Schwartz murmured and the Armstrongs were suddenly aware how deeply his face was grooved with pain, and remembered that he was a Viennese Jew, and had suffered in Dachau.

He replied to their inarticulate thoughts.

'In the camps, yes, it was terrible, but where else is there such cruelty, such prison, such domination? Shall I tell you? At times, in a good home, a good English home like little Jackson's.'

'Bloody horrible,' Abbott murmured, 'but the adoption's through now, you have complete care and custody of the child and what's more the old swine has to pay for his victim.'

'A righteous man, like Herr Himmler; a member of, what do they call it—The Strange Folk.'

'The Strange People,' said Simon, 'they can be the very devil! I know that from a couple of students.'

'The Devil, yes. It is He who comes when we let the

mind and will take over, and kill our feelings. I remember ...'

Schwartz looked through and away from them to the filthy cattle truck which had taken him from Vienna to Dachau. The camp in which his wife had died.

'It was on the "Death Train"; the more that perished on that trip, the better they liked it. Icy cold, it was, and in the truck one of my ... brethren, he was dying. An old man; it was not courage, I had gone past that. The train stopped for a moment—die Reglen—we had to wash in a freezing pool and relieve ourselves in the grasses. The SS boy saw Nathan lying in a corner, still; he had not obeyed the rule. He bent back to kick him in the stomach. "Stop," I say, "you cannot do this to an old man who is dying." For a moment he did stop and I saw grief, surprise, horror, all the feelings, all at once in that boy's face. Then his conditioning, the duty, slammed his face shut, and he hit me here.'

Simon felt for Laura's hand and pressed it as Dr Schwartz pointed to a small but deep cavity to the left of his mouth, 'that I do not mind, one must pay hard for a little wisdom, but as for old Nathan, he never got up from the frozen grasses. The old Jew, he had the good soul; for the SS boy, ach, what is the destiny? But Mark Jackson, he has made me remember; I must not make you sad, this is the good day. We must be glad, my friends, we must drink together ...'

'If you mean swig that horrible herbal stuff of yours, then count me out,' Abbott surfaced slowly from his friend's bitter memories.

'No, my dear Charles, you learn a little from me, from you I also learn. No herbs.'

Schwartz took a bottle of Scotch from a cupboard and filled three glasses. 'Let us drink, dear friends, not to the ... Yule Tide which is also upon us ...'

'With a nasty Hunnish reek too,' Abbott was still lost in his friend's story. 'I bet they hung more than coloured lights from those damn fir trees!'

'So it shall be to Rhoda and her new home on this planet.'

They drained their glasses and looked at Schwartz; so

much wisdom and a complete conviction as to reincarnation. As they walked upstairs to Rhoda's room, he patted Simon's shoulder.

'You, my dear Simon, are a young soul, you have not been so many times in the circles; Rhoda is only six but she is an old soul. Take no notice of that medicine man,' he smiled at Abbott, who had winked at Laura. 'You and Laura are the young souls, the soul of your daughter is old, that is very good, but it will be some time perhaps, before you understand me.'

Rhoda was nursing her doll. She did not move when they came into her bedroom, but her eyes were wide open and she was not asleep.

'Like flame,' thought Simon, looking at the child, 'flame taking its own form, the form is flame.'

'Hello, darling,' said Laura, 'here we are.'

Rhoda started and her doll dropped to the floor. 'Poor dolly,' she said.

'My pet, I'm so sorry,' Laura knelt down and picked up the broken toy.

Rhoda flung her arms round Mrs Armstrong. 'It's all right, it's only a doll.'

Schwartz nudged Simon. 'There, you see; the old soul!'

6

THERE was preparation for fun and games at Haydon Hall. It was Maria Theresa's birthday. Schwartz made an occasion of birthdays, believing, though he would not have put it this way, that they marked yet another stage in the temporal progression and purgation of an immortal soul. There were clusters of real candles round the dining room, and they lit up the paper designs which the children had fixed to the windows. At the centre of a large round table there was a cake with eight candles.

'Happy birthday to you, happy birthday to you,' a stout motherly woman struck up on the piano, accompanied on the flute by a long-haired youth—Dr Schwartz would have no canned music. 'Happy birthday to you,' the song was taken up by the whole gathering of children, spastics, psychotics, hydrocephalic idiots, mongols. They made up by vocal power what they lacked in melody. Only the autistic children were silent and solitary, though Dr Abbott noted with pleasure that some of them were craning forward with obvious interest, and moving their lips silently to the birthday song.

'Happy birthday dear Maria, happy birthday to you!' Simon and Laura had just got into the swing of it when the song rose to its climax, and with a slight creaking noise the heroine of the occasion was pushed forwards in a wheel chair. Simon felt Laura grip his hand, for the birthday girl lolled forward against the strap which kept her from falling, a loose tongue drooled from her lips and, although she was practically hairless, some enthusiast had wreathed her brow with a pink, bestarred ribbon.

'Ark, ark, ark,' gurgled this small scrap of desolate humanity as she was rolled through her birthday song to the cake at its centre. The candles were lit for her, and Maria Theresa drooped forward to their flickering points of flame.

'As if, not knowing, she did know the meaning of all this,'

thought Laura, remembering the ghost and the machine.

The birthday song ended, much to the disappointment of the mongol brigade, who could have done with another hour of it. Rhoda was happily holding Laura's hand; Dr Schwartz bent down and whispered to her, 'Be a love and ask Maria what she would like for her special song.'

The Armstrong's new daughter skipped forward to the wheel chair and whispered to Maria Theresa, who stumbled out some wordless sound. Rhoda came back to Schwartz. 'I thought so, Luke,' she said, 'it's Pop goes the Weasel.'

When they talked about it later, Abbott and the Armstrongs recalled the drama and significance of the scene. It was the Pied Piper but this time the little lame boy was in the procession.

Ta, tata, tata, tata, the motherly pianist trod out the tune. The long-haired flautist came down from the stage and with no scrap of self-consciousness, started to caper round the hall fluting gaily. The children, except for the autistics, followed him, singing:

> 'Up and down the city road,
> In and out the Eagle,
> That's the way the money goes,
> Pop goes the Weasel.'

First came a gaggle of uproarious mongols mingled with a variety of defectives and a small boy with an appalling external tumour, who had tried to kill his baby brother. They whooped and leapt with glee to be real members of a real group, participating. The polio cases levered themselves forward on aluminium crutches, or were pushed in chairs, Maria Theresa among them. Then came the 'difficult' and 'deprived' children, Rhoda with them, rather sedate and detached but singing happily.

'The man's a bloody genius,' Abbott murmured to Laura, as, behind their Pied Piper, the rout jumbled past them, 'recidivists, psychotics, not to mention his mongols and floor-tappers, all communicating. How the hell does he do it?'

The music stopped and Dr Schwartz walked into the centre of the hall.

'That was fine, my dears, that was lovely to see and listen to. In a moment tea'—the mongols applauded loudly. 'Yes, tea and then a little play and some games with your older friends and myself. But first, three cheers for our birthday girl, three cheers for Maria Theresa.'

When the cheering stopped, the children trooped into the dining room and much to the Armstrongs' surprise, stood or sat at their places in silence. Dr Schwartz stood at the end of the table and bowed his head.

'Blessed be this meal, blessed be the earth from which comes our bread, blessed be the waters, blessed be all men, women and children, blessed be all living creatures, for they also are brothers and sisters, blessed be this meal.'

As they sat down, Schwartz looked at his watch. 'Almost six o'clock, opening time, my old friend, still tea it is for a little while longer.'

'Don't bother about the time, I'm delighted to miss a pint or two when I can see your work in progress; still, a glass of your Scotch wouldn't come amiss before the charades get going.'

'Your machine has need of the petrol?'

'How well you put it,' Abbott grinned, 'it certainly does, if I'm going to do a turn at your fun and games. I remember last year.'

'When you were Mother Goose! Of that they talked for many days.'

'I can still remember,' Abbott pretended to shudder. 'But Luke, no wonder they gave you that name, how the hell do you do it? I had a good look round. Twenty-five per cent of your children would be confined and under constant sedation if they were in some of the health resorts I've been to.'

'I and my colleagues, you too Charles, and my dear Armstrongs, we know the soul; that knowing, it is, which brings, ach, forgive the word, the love. To know, it is the same in some languages as to love?'

'In Hebrew, I think, but with some slight reservations as to the brand of loving,' said Simon.

'Still,' said Luke, 'it is that. Also we must keep close to feelings, to the Nature.'

'And some of my techniques,' said Charles, thinking of the pills he had prescribed for little Jackson.

'Yes, I am becoming more "with it". One must use everything that is in tune with the Nature, but for me, evil can bring good,' again Dr Schwartz stared into the darkness. 'For me there is always Dachau.'

Tea was soon over and after another short grace the children went back to the hall and Schwartz took his guest to his study.

'Up to the top, please,' said Abbott as Luke began to fill his glass.

'So, the curer of souls still has need of the artificial stimulus, tch, tch!'

'Artificial my foot, I don't see why Mother Nature shouldn't take credit for such excellent whisky.'

'Both true and an excellent rationalisation,' Schwartz gasped as Abbott drained his tumbler of whisky at one gulp. 'But you I know, my old friend, when you drink like that, something is on your mind.'

'Trying to come into my mind—has been all the afternoon, but I'm not as tough as you. I can't think clearly after all that birthday racket, much as I approve of it.'

'Then we leave you for a moment while you get busy with your thoughts. Come, my friends, I know Charles.'

They moved away from the sideboard.

'For a man like him who is of the intellect and the imagination, it is not always easy. Now he dissolves the intellect a little so that the imagination can have its say.'

'He certainly does.' Simon could glimpse in the mirror that Dr Abbott was filling his third tumbler.

'You noticed at our party. I know just a little, but it is your Rhoda who can best speak to and understand little Maria. It is not the reading of the lips. No, it is some other sense, some other way of knowing. Our birthday girl has the hardest Karma. She is not only what you can see, but a deaf mute.'

'Well, chaps, I'm ready for the fray if you are.' After his fourth tumbler Dr Abbott had not only uncreased but was glowing with excitement and good humour.

'And the problem?'

45

'We shall see,' said Charles, as they followed Dr Schwartz back to the party.

A play of Red Riding Hood by staff and children was near its climax.

'What big eyes you've got!'

'All the better to see you with.'

The children were tense with excitement and the mongols could not hold back benevolent advice and comment.

'Watch out, silly girl, it's Wolfy,' shouted one as Red Riding Hood tip-toed with her basket of presents to the figure in bed with its long papier-mâché nose, flop ears and woolly nightcap.

'What big teeth you've got!'

'All the better to eat you with.'

There was a gasp of horror as Grandma Wolf leapt out of bed and crouched, ready to plunge, before Red Riding Hood. But Simon and Laura noticed that when the wood-cutter arrived and dispatched the wolf with a couple of swift axe blows, the response was by no means unequivocal. They remembered how Schwartz had said 'they are all feeling but no intellect, they can teach us to feel again,' for a Mongol was in tears.

'Poor Wolfy,' he sobbed, 'poor Wolfy.'

Some games came next and they remarked with what tact and expertise Dr Schwartz's colleagues—he would not refer to them as staff—helped their handicapped charges to participate.

During the pause for lemonade and ices, Abbott whispered to Luke who nodded agreement and walked to the centre of the hall.

'Children, do you remember at our last party somebody who played at being Mother Goose?'

There was a pause, as those children who had them searched their minds and memory, then:

'Yes, Mother Goose.'

The affirmation grew in volume.

'Goose, Mother Goose, we want Goosey.' The applause was joined by the discordant voices of some who had no clue what it was all about, but liked to be in the swim.

Slowly Dr Abbott walked to his friend at the centre of

the hall, bowed to right and left, raised his arms, waggled them in mimic flight, stuck out his neck, and very solemnly emitted an impeccable 'quack-quack'.

In the tumult of applause that followed, Simon muttered to Laura, 'That alone deserves a few Scotches.'

'You wait,' she said, 'he's only warming up.'

'Friends, children,' Charles hammered it out in the grand style, 'once again I am happy to be with you at a splendid party and salute dear Maria Theresa on her special day. The last time I came—it was as Mother Goose, and I was so glad you liked my performance. This evening I shall be a goose again—to start with, and then something else, but I need one of you to help me.'

With some difficulty Dr Schwartz hushed the crowd who had leapt up, raring to go. It was a put-up job. He bent down and whispered to Rhoda who pulled her jersey straight and walked smiling to Dr Abbott. He bowed solemnly.

'Ah, Rhoda has come to my aid. Children, Rhoda and I are going to pretend we are people who turn into birds.'

'How can he do it,' Laura whispered to Simon, for the eminent psychiatrist had started to walk round the centre of the hall with the exact neck-jerking and stilted steps of a heron. Rhoda followed him, but the Armstrongs noted with pleasure that she was not only following Abbott imitating a heron, but making good-natured fun of his imitation. Abbott also realised it and shouting 'Ducks' squatted down and began to honk and quack and flap.

'And to hell with inhibitions,' thought Simon as to tumultuous applause his old friend reared his behind to heaven and began to dab for little fish and tadpoles on the floor of Haydon Hall. Rhoda followed his example, but thank goodness, thought the Armstrongs, with considerably less abandon. Then Abbott got to his feet and spoke quietly and more seriously to the silent children.

'Now Rhoda and I are going to try something a bit more difficult. You remember Little Miss Muffet?'

'Yes,' shouted some members of his audience.

'Then what was little Miss Muffet frightened of?'

'Spiders.'

47

'Quite right.' Dr Abbott stopped as a small boy with the horribly swollen head of a hydrocephalic idiot staggered to his feet and recited with an effort comparable to, and of as great value, as the ascent of the final crack of Katchenjunga:

> 'There came a big spider
> And sat down beside her
> And frightened Miss Muffet away.'

Schwartz and Abbott led the applause.

'Thank you, Roddy,' said Abbott, 'that was very good indeed.'

'More than good,' thought Laura, 'considering the instrument he has got to play on.'

'What else are we frightened of?'

Of all the adults present only Schwartz was undisturbed by his friend's direct assault on his children, who one way or another had been very frightened indeed.

'What else are we frightened of? Try and tell Luke; now I am frightened of rats.'

'Not rats, Daddies,' it was the voice of little Jackson that seeped through the silence.

'Mummies and Daddies.'

'Mummies and Daddies, not rats, not spiders . . . Mummies.'

Evidently Abbott thought his loosening up process had gone far enough.

'We're all frightened of something, but when we grow up we often see there was no need to be afraid of what we were frightened of. Now, let's think of people who are frightened of bats.'

Armstrong felt a slight tightening of the scalp; so that was what Charles was getting at.

'Really most bats are very nice little creatures, they are gentle and delicate, they eat lots of nasty insects, they fly beautifully, they can see in the darkness. But . . . well, I am going to be a horrid bat and we will find out whether Rhoda is frightened of me.'

The Armstrongs smiled as their future daughter's light clear voice announced:

'They sleep upside down, you know, you'll have to hang

upside down from the ceiling if you are going to start the game properly.'

'But this bat is awake already, because it's dusk, you see.'

The children looked out at the cypress trees, very dark in the gathering twilight. There were no blinds or curtained windows at Haydon Hall.

'Yes, it's dusk now, but I'm going to put Rhoda in a safe little house so that no bat can hurt her.'

Abbott took a piece of chalk out of his pocket, bent down and drew a circle round Laura.

'Now love, you must imagine that chalk circle is your house. Stay in it or "Woof!" I'll get you.'

Rhoda smiled at Abbott. 'Bats don't say "Woof", but they do start off each evening by hanging upside down from their toes.'

Luke bent down to Simon and Laura. 'You see what I mean, she has the old soul.'

Abbott vanished. The children sat in complete silence, only Rhoda stood upright at the centre of her chalk circle; from some far corner there came a long thin half scream, half whistle. It was followed by twittering and chirping.

'That's not a bird,' Simon's dream returned, the thick fleshy leaves, the noseless face, the same twittering. He felt a hand on his shoulder.

'Believe me, Simon,' said Dr Schwartz, 'Charles does know what he's up to.'

He needed the reassurance, that dream had disturbed him deeply.

'Christ!' thought Laura, 'Charles has made good use of that whisky!' He was bent double and his face and shoulders were covered with black, lacy stuff held across them by penetrating thumbs. It was too true for it to be real to them. The children, those who could make noises, screamed with terror and delight as Dr Charles Abbott, MD, DPsy, DPM weaved over the floor which was now all sky and forest, darting hither and thither after imaginary insects but always in narrowing circles after his real prey—Rhoda.

At last he reached the chalk circle. He stood up and hissed, he bent down and with one hand tried to scrabble the chalk.

49

'Twinkle, twinkle, little bat. How I wonder what you're at,' said Rhoda as she brought the heel of her shoe hard down on Abbott's fingers.

'Ouch!' said the eminent psychiatrist as he got up, grinning with pain and pleasure, 'that hurt, but,' he turned to his friends, 'Professor and Mrs Armstrong, you're on to a good thing, the point is what you make of it.'

Dr Schwartz murmured, 'Now, you see what I mean, the old soul, the already understanding.'

Rhoda looked at her new parents and sighed, 'I'm so sleepy, shall we go home now?'

7

'SHE CERTAINLY enjoys the brothers Grimm,' Simon smiled at his wife, who was busy making a frock for their new daughter. Rhoda had been with them for a month now and these bed-time stories were part of her rhythm.

'She wants the real stuff,' said Laura, screwing up her eyes to thread a needle and thinking of the Sleeping Beauty. 'I tried her on a snappy modern number last night and was told it wasn't a "proper story"; she was quite right too.'

'Interesting how they like Grimm although he's so savage. He interprets their own problems. I wasn't allowed the stuff when I was a kid.'

'Unluckily for you. Don't you be too easy with her, darling, I mean when she does her "Just one more and then I'll settle" stunt. If you do she'll get to be the Dictator and you'll be full of bottled-up fury.'

Laura knew her husband and that he had not really caught up with the change that Rhoda had made in their lives.

The telephone bell rang. Simon lifted the receiver and was greeted by the explosion which Abbott thought appropriate for the instrument.

'Armstrong? Abbott.'

'Yes, Charles. What are you cooing about?'

'How about a pint at The Rover? I want to fix up a meeting with the Johnson girl, she's at one of her crises—vampire speaking.'

'Right, I'll be round in five minutes.'

'It's Abbott, love, he wants to have a talk with me at The Rover about that Stella Johnson. You remember, Dracula's protegée.'

'Of course I remember.' Laura wondered why her husband was hedging uncertainly. 'You'd better get off then, it should be interesting.'

'All right, all right, I'm going. Not the least chance of

you joining us, I suppose, not nowadays.'

Laura began to cough. 'Wish I could but that's out of the question. How long will you be?'

'As long as I damn well please.' The thought of her anxiety at his petulance only irritated him and he slammed the door noisily.

'He certainly has some way to go before he adjusts to a threesome,' Laura thought when she was alone. 'Have we really got enough that's strong and positive between us? I used to think so; perhaps it's only a question of time. And Rhoda's so quick at understanding. On walks, for instance, with him it's always talking to me on one level, then ignoring me and chatting to the girl. She knows it and does all she can to bridge the gap, she succeeds too, we were together as a family the other day and honest to God it was thanks to her.'

She remembered how Rhoda had for a while insisted on holding both their hands and being swung, how she had brought them both into her excited observation of coot and mallard on the lake.

'I know it's good for all three of us, that he was ready for a child and we can all grow together. He's got enough confidence now to share me with a daughter.'

She reached automatically for a cigarette and lit it, remembering how years ago when she had been pregnant, her husband had started a series of petty affairs as if he could not bear the withdrawal of her pregnancy and must have the reassurance of someone who seemed for himself alone. She remembered with pain and a faint whisper of present anxiety, but brushed it aside like a web.

'No, that's all over now, he really has got out of some of his childish uncertainty.'

She touched her side as she thought of Rhoda sleeping in her small white room and smiled as if a gap had at long last been filled, then turned on the news and got on with her dress-making.

Abbott was already at The Rover, scowling at two overfed and dressy women who were gushing over a long-suffering poodle.

He looked up when Simon entered, 'Well, how's things?'

'Fine, why do you ask?' said Armstrong defensively.

'Don't be so naïve, you've just adopted a child and of course I'm interested in how it's going. Anyway, hang on while I get you a pint.'

'Surprisingly well,' said Simon, when his friend returned, 'of course I know there are difficulties in making a three-some, after years of just the two of us. But I'm really fond of Rhoda, and she's got surprising insight, does wonders for Laura and me.'

'Fine, the "old soul" as old Schwartz put it. Just keep close to your real feelings and not too much of the lovey-dovey stuff and it should be a real asset to your marriage. Laura is very maternal and she'll be all the better for you if she has a child.'

'Rhoda's certainly taken to family life.'

'She wanted it. An institution isn't a home, even if it's run by Schwartz. That child is strong—you know, emotionally. I'm not referring to our rock-climbing. Incidentally, that's a first-rate outlet for aggression. I could do with a few climbs myself. When are you going down to that Welsh cottage of yours?'

'Next week.'

'If it's OK with you, I'll try and join you. One can get pretty satiated sitting in a chair listening to patients.'

'That would be marvellous. I really would like it Charles.'

'That's a date then, but it may depend on Miss Stella Johnson. By the way, she's the one I wanted to talk to you about.'

'How is she?'

'Less batty,' Dr Abbott grinned approvingly at his pun. 'One of my PSWs caught her making up in the mirror, so she must be seeing that pretty face of hers again. Incidentally, I've got to go round to the clinic in a few moments, can you come with me?'

Simon hesitated, thinking of Laura. 'There's nothing I would like more, but I should be reading some Finals papers.'

'See the world in a grain of sand. You know quite well

a look that's quick does the trick, or you wouldn't have time to write those books of yours.'

'Right, Charles, just one more pint and I'm with you.'

'We must be there before eight,' said Abbott, when Simon returned with the drinks. 'Stella is leading a brisk social life these days. Ever heard of the Melting Pot?'

'You mean Daphne's place?' Simon remembered the stout and asp-tongued Madame who presided over a drinking club in Soho, the piano, the shadowy clientèle. 'Don't tell me she's patronising that hell-hole!'

'She certainly is, and hell-hole's the right word for the place. I went down the other night to see what's it's like.'

'I'm not particularly squeamish, but that gang really do give me a belly ache.'

'Apparently I wasn't dressed for the part. She has a nice way of taking coats: "Just let me take that bit of old tat." ' Not for the first time Simon was surprised by his friend's histrionic gift—he had reproduced Daphne's patronising drawl to the life.

'Can't have you about the place in that nonsense, not even with Stella. No pints dear, sorry, only shorties. This isn't a beer house. Yes, fifteen shillings is quite correct for two whiskeys, you pay for the atmosphere.'

'That's Daphne, but Charles, why do you let your patient go to that *dump*?'

'How could I stop her, even if I believed in stopping and didn't know Stella has to go her own way? Also Madame has got a crush on the girl. But no, I don't stop people, only try and let a bit of light on the scene. Well, let's be off or Stella will have gone to The Melting Pot.'

8

SIMON felt anxious as Abbott knocked at the door of Stella's room in the expensive nursing home. He knew that his capacity for projecting Helens of Troy on to various women had been unlimited and he hoped that Stella would be plain and disagreeable. His wish was not granted. The girl who welcomed them was both elegant and self-possessed.

'Charles, Simon! I may call you Simon, Professor Armstrong? I know your work so well it would be silly to stick to surnames. Now, what will you drink? Beer like Charles, or will you have gin or vodka?'

'If possible, beer for each of us and none of your Bloody Marys.'

'But why,' Stella smiled at Simon, 'do they only use your poem "Refugees" in the anthologies? There are so many others just as good.'

'I suppose because it's in the Golden Treasury and anthologists don't draw from new books of verse, but from the other anthologies.'

'I see, a kind of literary incest.'

'Literary incest!' Simon started; he had used that phrase on numerous occasions. Perhaps it was part of the sense he had of having met Stella before, of innumerable meetings.

She filled up two pewter mugs. 'Beer for you and Simon and for me a vodka and tomato juice. I can . . . regulate my drinks now. No doubt Charles—he is quite unprofessional —has told you that I was a compulsive alcoholic.'

Abbott pointed his cigar at Simon. ' "Compulsive Alcoholic" is what we call someone who drinks more than ourselves. Anyway the bard was one, back in the roaring thirties.'

'So that also we have in common.'

Charles frowned and exhaled a cloud of ferocious smoke. 'Everybody has a great deal in common, even psychopaths and spinsters in Slough. But all drinkers are potential alcoholics, it's a question of thinking the next drink ahead.

Always we must feel, and always we must know our feelings.'

Stella looked at Simon with narrowed slanting eyes. '*The Cult of the Vampire?* I read your article and I was fascinated. Doubtless Charles has told you about my other trouble.'

'Of course I have, sorry.' Abbott stamped out the glowing tip of his cigar ash on the immaculate golden carpet and Simon noted with pleasure that Stella was quite unmoved by the dark stain although she did pass over an ashtray.

'Yes, I have, Simon knows a few things about vampires that neither you nor I do. As for telling, I've no time for bogus privacy. We aren't neat little capsules of private "meness". More like a spider's web, centres of being but interconnected; touch any part of the net and the whole fabric quivers.'

Stella sipped her drink and remarked softly, 'I agree, but some of these centres must be nearer together than others, their mutual vibrations must be stronger, more vivid.'

'Vivid's the word,' thought Simon, 'the woman glitters.'

'But my "vampire phobia"; some time after I came to Charles, you must believe this, I couldn't see my face in a mirror, or if...'

'Or if—go on, I haven't heard this,' said Abbott.

'I think it happened twice, I've only just remembered, perhaps it's your both being here makes me strong enough ... it was terrifying.'

'Go on,' said Abbott, leaning forward eagerly.

'Yes, I did see something in the glass. First there were thick fleshy leaves in front of me but I seemed to be among them. I could hear things, little rustlings and twittering. I was in a jungle. Then one column of light with insects fluttering in it pierced through the foliage like a path of dusty brightness. It was then I saw the creature ... Oh God!'

'Go on, love,' murmured Abbott, 'you're with us now.'

'It slid down the light towards me and its face was grey, grey wrinkled skin with a thatch of reddish hair. It had a nose like a kind of triangular leaf with open, flat nostrils. Its mouth was open and I could see its yellow teeth and how it had no chin, only a lump of twisted moving muscles, moving under the skin like cords. Get me a drink, Simon.'

She swallowed the vodka that he gave her at one gulp and went on, her eyes fixed on the vision which he knew only too well.

'It came right up to me and I could smell its breath like rotten meat. Then it began to speak directly to my mind, there were no words and its fingers, they were like a child's only spikey and hard, fumbled at the buttons of my dress. It was bending towards my neck. "Believe on me, and you will have peace, peace. I will drink your blood, you will drink my blood then you will hunger and thirst no more." I couldn't have held out but then, then another light started, following down the shaft, and the light took the face of a child, very calm, very strong. It seemed to melt through the face of the creature so that I could see through it. I remember how the vampire, it must have been that, seemed to congeal for one second in a spasm of intense hatred then it vanished into nothing and I was looking at my own face in the mirror.'

They sat silently for a moment, Stella looking calm and relaxed after she had relived her vision of evil.

There was the rasp of Abbott's match, and a blue spurt in the twilight.

'So that's how it happened, that's how you started to see yourself again. Am I glad you've been able to recapture all this, relive it.'

'So am I, I feel as if I've uncreased, as if a tumour had melted away inside me.'

'It probably has. You can see your face in a mirror now, judging by your charming make-up. But why so smart? Don't tell me you're off to the Melting Pot again?'

Stella sucked in her lower lip and turned petulantly towards Simon.

'Do you agree with Charles that the Melting Pot is a witch's kitchen? That's if you've ever been there?'

'Yes,' Armstrong gave a mock shudder, 'I've been there and I certainly agree with Charles. But I only went there to meet John Chester. Does he still go there?'

'So you know my John.' Simon smiled at the possessive adjective.

Chester was a New Zealand sculptor whose parents had known only sheep, but he was of international fame. He had trapped with a terrifying exactness the stress of man dominated by the machine, by some religious code, some orthodox pattern of behaviour, and then slowly bursting apart in climax after climax of hysteria. In his sparse, tortured shapes he had bodied forth the hell of his century. He was hermaphrodite, and one of the most significant artists of his age. But he went the solitary way of his art and his perversion and—'*my* John'!—he was owned by no one.

'Yes, years ago I used to know him very well. But he became a bit too off-beat even for me, and I had no relish for his "camp" followers. We parted and so ended my liaison with the Melting Pot. Does that Daphne still run the place?'

'I told you she does,' growled Abbott, 'and she's a real vulture, seven and six for a whisky!'

'Oh, I admit she's a monster, darling, but she has quality.'

Simon started again: 'quality'! That was Chester's word for most of his unpleasant women friends.

'I mean she lives very near the nerve.'

Chester again. 'The woman's a sponge,' Simon thought. Stella had not only used two of Chester's favourite phrases, but had expressed them with the exact qualities of his cold ironic drawl.

Abbott scowled. 'I've only got you off booze and bat phobias for a few days and you become a Melting Pot addict.'

'You come with me tonight,' said Stella to Simon, 'then I'll be well chaperoned and Charles won't need to grumble.'

For a few seconds he hesitated; he would have loved to be with her. Then he thought of Laura.

'Sorry, no go for this evening, I have a date.'

'Then tomorrow, Chester's sure to come; I do want you to be there. Please come.'

'I'll think about it,' said Simon as the door bell rang.

'Good, good. I'll meet you at about eight. That's my taxi. "Now where's my mink?" as Daphne would put it. Charles, say you're not cross or I'll be miserable all the evening.'

'I don't give a damn provided you stay reasonably sane.

But don't let that Daphne creature drain you dry; seven and six for a glass of whisky!'

'Half a crown for me,' said Stella, as she slid out of the room, 'I can deal with her.'

For a few moments after Stella had swept off, they sat smoking; then very deliberately Simon turned to Abbott.

'I had not expected this.'

'You mean Stella's vision. I think you helped her to come out with it; something to do with that spider's web and closeness of meeting. You see why I wanted you to meet? She'll be a lot freer with that horror brought into daylight.'

'There's more to it than that.'

'You mean . . . ?'

'The night after my lecture I had a dream—this is the point—it resembled in almost every detail what Stella has just told us.'

Abbott's cigar glowed sharply in the dusk. 'Did it now? You're not fitting in bits—was it exact?'

'There is a complete correspondence.'

'I suppose it's surprising that we should be surprised. Since we both believe in diabolic possession there's no unearthly reason why two people shouldn't be possessed by the same devils, have a vision of the same archetype. After all, it's common enough, in religion; lots of Christians have almost identical visions of Christ; and I suppose those desert fathers wrestled with the same succubi. It's when it happens here and now that we are astonished, still it's good for our theories to be bodied out in fact.'

Simon reached for another beer, opened it and filled his tankard.

'It certainly gave me a shock. Her dream was identical.'

'It will fill out your metaphors. Well, good luck if you go to The Melting Pot and try and put those whiskeys on your expense account. Stella can tell you a lot about vampires. But do try to get her into more satisfying company than that club, it would help; you know lots of reasonably sane people, and that's what she needs. Well, I must be off, got a string of patients in the morning.'

As he walked home through the river mist, Simon found himself repeating a stanza from *In Memoriam*,

A hand that can be clasped no more
Behold me for I cannot sleep
And like a guilty thing I creep
At earliest morning to the door.

Laura was waiting up to meet him. 'Well, how did it go?'
she asked, a trifle anxiously for her husband was not adept
at concealing his feelings. 'What is she like?'

Simon slumped into a chair and kicked his shoes off. He
poured them a drink, then brooded for some seconds.
'Well, Rider Haggard's *She*—illustrated by Aubrey Beards-
ley and edited—very smoothly edited. Incidentally "She
who must be obeyed" has already issued an invitation. Can
we both meet her at The Melting Pot tomorrow evening?'

'Anything for you love, although you know what I think
of that hell-hole.'

'I can't stand the place either but Charles thinks it's a
question of our helping to winkle her out of it and introducing her to some different company.'

'Well, I'll have to get a baby sitter and it's out of term.'

'Nothing simple any more,' Simon grumbled, 'I really
do want you to come with me. I really do!'

'Do you really want simplicity? But I'll do my very best,
I'll rustle up someone tomorrow, never fear.'

As Laura poised on the edge of sleep, a vision of the bay
of a Welsh sea-coast soothed her, and over the long wave-
ribbed sand she heard the piping of dunlin and oyster-
catchers, saw zig-zagging snipe and the long down-fluting
flight of curlew.

But later in the night she prodded her husband. She had
been woken by the sound of his teeth grinding, steadily
grinding.

9

LAURA replaced the receiver for the fifth time. 'Sorry darling, but that's the final refusal; they're all going to a Christmas binge. It looks as if The Melting Pot is off as far as I'm concerned.'

Professor Armstrong glared into his coffee cup and Laura remarked that no one could register despair with such telling effect as her husband.

'What are your plans?'

There was a long sagging silence. 'Examiners' Board in the morning and then I've got some new students to interview with the Master of Unity, you know that fellow, he ignores the students except to tell every one of them his ghastly life story.'

'From pit miner's cottage to the Mastership of this ancient college. Darling, what a bore for you!'

'It is; I have to get a few answers from the dazed creatures while he takes a cat nap. It will be at least six before we knock off, so I thought I'd . . .'

'Yes, darling?' Laura realised that her husband had already decided and was hedging guiltily.

'Well, exorcise the vampire I told you about, at The Melting Pot—for an hour or so.'

'Try and make it more an hour than a "so",' said Laura bleakly, 'we'll miss you.'

'Tell Rhoda I'll give her an extra session tomorrow evening, that's a promise. Goodbye darling.'

Professor Armstrong drove off to the university.

'He's in quite a hurry to be off,' Laura lit a cigarette and began to cough over it. 'No petulance now, when I can't come. Am I going to lose after all? I can't believe it, and Charles is so sure that there's nothing to worry about.'

The Melting Pot had been a lucrative but by no means swinging Soho drinking club until, inspired by a common passion for chemin de fer, John Chester met Daphne Clauberg in Monte Carlo. She had impressed him from the start and John would often recall their first meeting.

'It was about six o'clock m'dears, just think of that! I'd done rather well on the tables, and you know how marvellous it is when you have a run on the wheel—a kind of orgasm. Well, I came back to the hotel to powder my nose and have a rinse and there on the next balcony was Daphne. Stinkers and Starkers as they say in Maidenhead, and Daphne without a stitch is quite something. She goes out and in more flamboyantly than most and in all the wrong places. But you see,' Chester's voice grew husky and serious, for him it had been an aesthetic experience— 'the flies, they had settled all over her cunt and were feeding. They buzzed and she snored, over the main boulevard, mind you, buzz, snore. Dear Daphne, she doesn't wear a mask, and it's very rare to meet someone who lives so close to the nerve. Mind you, I never listen to a word the silly cow says, but she does live which is more than I can say for you silly trollops.'

The monologue would explode in high-pitched male laughter, enhanced by Daphne Clauberg's deep-chested gurgling baritone. She had reasons to be fond of John. He was faithful to her club and it had become the centre of an ever increasing circle not only of wealthy and 'strange' sensation hunters, but distinguished artists and patrons of the arts. For under the paternal frippery of John Chester was his genius. It was infernal and of particular relevance to this present day, it was his closest companion, and it was as tough as steel. Indeed, when in serious mood Chester allowed his splendid talent to break cover, he could make the stoutest critic or heterosexual interviewer dwindle into candy floss.

'His perversion feeds his talent,' Simon had often thought when his one-time friend limped into The Melting Pot battered after some protracted, masochistic session with a bogus coal-heaver. But if in some curious way Chester's perversion fed his talent, both of them nourished Daphne. As her wealthy customers gathered she had steadily increased her prices until her shabbier clientele took off for less costly haunts.

She had also enhanced her decor. Negresses, nude, ebony but discreetly Westernised, held pink electric torches to the satin draped ceiling. One side of the room was covered with heavy embossed paper. It simulated a tropical wall. There were mossy stones, brilliant fungi, and a plentiful supply of emerald lizards. There was also a stuffed alligator on the grand piano where a vast African pianist in an immaculate white dinner jacket vamped out the melodies of Noel Coward and Cole Porter.

'Infinitely superior to chrome, off-white stipple and green vomit,' Chester would murmur, 'at least Daphne has the courage of her convictions and they are far too awful to be vulgar.'

One thing he did insist on. There was a neon sign over the door of The Melting Pot, but the original dank, unlit and perilous stairway remained. Simon had once thought it was some unexpected sentiment of his friend, a sense of period and contrast. He knew better now; on a number of occasions at the closing time of midnight, he had seen the sculptor standing at the doorway. As some wealthy, artistic-ally-inclined stockbroker whom he had persuaded to drink far too much gin plunged headlong down this via dolorosa, he had licked his lips with relish.

'Simon,' said the famous New Zealander, 'isn't it just too marvellous to see them on all fours?'

When Armstrong arrived, The Melting Pot was humming like a beehive and as usual John Chester was the queen.

'Goodness!' he gave a little shriek as he saw Simon. 'If it isn't the only heterosexual poet in South-West London! That's much more queer than us girls.'

As he glided towards him, Simon thought, 'he hasn't forgiven our unpleasant parting and he hasn't forgotten our ... friendship.' He remembered how his friend had expected their relationship to drift over into direct sexuality and how, though attracted, he had found it impossible to make love to someone with bristles and a penis.

'And why have you returned to your vomit, darling, after all these years, don't tell me you're after me again?'

'Simon,' it was Stella sitting primly at the bar, Daphne

leaning towards her with an air of ownership.

'Simon,' Chester hissed, 'what's the name of that favourite old queen of yours? Gentle Jesus! don't tell me you've been hooked by that little culture-vulture!'

'Not hooked,' said Simon, waving to Stella and rather pleased at the sculptor's comment—he might prove as effective an exorcist as Laura. 'Just interested.'

'Well, you can be interested in me now and stop your pranks. Daphne love, champagne all round on the Reverend Armstrong.'

Simon fought back the passivity that Chester could induce.

'Sorry, but you're drinking gin and I'll replenish, but you can buy your own champagne; by all accounts you're as rich as Croesus.'

Chester clapped his hands and drawled, 'Daphne, champagne for us all on the Reverend.'

'Champagne on the vicar, champers on the vicar,' Chester's request was taken up as a refrain by his entourage; rouged and spiteful they mobbed round Simon.

Oh God, he thought, Laura, the newspapers, don't let me go off the deep end, hit one of these little bastards.

'It's just like a Greek play,' Chester said, 'Orpheus among the Maenads, a bit mixed up sexually, my dears, but who isn't? Shall we tear him for his bad verses?'

'Champagne, champers, champagne,' Simon's eyes misted over with a familiar redness, and his stomach tensed with excitement. He stretched his hand like a blade and looked for the right spot on the neck of the middle-aged museum curator with bleached hair who was pulling his tie.

'Watch it, girls,' screeched Chester; he was a mere interested spectator now the hunt was up, 'the bard is getting temperkins.'

Simon felt someone poke at his anus with a hard thumb. He bent forward, placed both hands on the bar counter and kicked backwards. The Maenads withdrew in silence. Gordon Stonham, the art cirtic, was doubled up on the pile carpet, clutching his winded belly and gasping.

Chester pretended to be delighted. 'Always liven up the place, you old bore you. But I haven't pardoned you yet.

Daphne, champagne on the Vicar.'

'Champagne nothing.'

'If you must come here, then you can behave like a human being to my friends.' Chester raised his glass and flung it at Simon's face. He jerked his head aside and heard the glass splinter on the tropic wall.

'Well done, Mr Chester, you've killed one of Aunty's pretty lizards, "congratters" as your pals would say.'

Simon uncreased as he felt Stella's hand on his shoulder.

'Sorry love,' she said, 'I wouldn't have asked you here if I'd known you'd get into this nonsense.'

'Little female shit, poxed-up ninny.' Chester spat out the words and for the second time in his life, Simon saw his one-time friend without his panzoid gloss, and without his talent; nothing but the venom.

'Look at this little cunt,' he rallied his bewildered followers.

'O Mr Chester, how d'you do,
Your nice sculptures ring so true.'

He spat at Stella and the lump was grey on the gold carpet.

'I think it's about time you went home to your loony bin and took your vicar with you.'

The pianist who was also the strong arm man came forward.

'No, my pet,' Daphne wavered between her loyalty to Chester and her crush on Stella. The crush won.

'Not tonight, Nigel darling.' Reluctantly and still glowering at Armstrong, the pianist returned to his stool.

'We don't really want the nasty police in and our names in the dailies, do we darlings?'

The sculptor had calmed down now but looked with some unease at Stella who was sipping at her gin. He was not used to having his authority questioned.

'The champagne's on me, loves,' boomed Daphne, in her role of peacemaker, 'and what's more, my honey-lambs, Stella will pour out the bubbly, won't you baby?'

Chester and his party teetered a few silent moments over their champagne and then trailed off to fresh pastures. The

65

Melting Pot would be a bore for many nights to come.

Simon sat down by Stella. 'I hadn't expected all this.'

'You don't suit their stomachs, particularly poor John's.'

'Why poor John? He was spoiling for a row.'

'He'd have been delighted to see you if it hadn't been for me,' Stella smiled. 'Old friendships die hard; particularly ambiguous ones.'

Simon brooded for a moment remembering the closeness of that old relationship.

'You're half right; but Stella, I once learnt a lot from that man.'

'Of course, darling, but now isn't it time for deady, I mean beddy-byes.'

Daphne's eyes glinted maliciously from their padded sockets.

Medusa in person, Simon clicked his fingers to be sure they were still mobile and looked more closely. A smudge of lipstick reddened her teeth and, yes, the woman must shave; even in this light, that was five o'clock shadow.

'Rude to stare,' Daphne snapped Simon out of his field-work, 'and, once more, it's your beddy-byes.'

'What are you up to?' asked Stella. 'Have another drink and relax.'

'Dear little Stella, you're always right and—goodness, aren't you attractive!' Daphne winked massively. She put an enormous arm round Stella's shoulders and grinned at Simon. 'But it is girls' talk now, darling, and two's company; shoo!'

Stella nestled under the enormous arm; then she looked at Simon, her half-shut eyes opened, and flicked through the 'mummy's girl' expression which had clouded them.

'For Christ's sake,' she said, 'be your age, woman, Professor Armstrong came here because I asked him!'

The quiver which, seeming to rise out of the floor, shook Miss Clauberg's body, would have registered on a seismograph. The pianist stopped playing and looked enquiringly at his employer.

'Oh, calm down darling.'

Daphne registered the endearment. She glanced sideways at Stella, she wobbled for a moment, then Niagara took

66

over from Vesuvius and she poured her slackening body over the counter.

'She's out to get her,' thought Simon, as silvered finger-nails curved outwards. 'The act's quite deliberate but it may do the trick if it touches off the girl's "Mater Dolorosa" nonsense; I ought to know that well enough.'

'People are such bores, I can't stand them, but us two darling, we're different, and you know you're so terribly attractive. We could be such friends, and you know I haven't got any real friends, only let's pretend ones. They don't want me, only my money.'

'That's quite something,' he grinned to himself, 'with her gin at seven and six a nip, but she's softening up Miss Johnson; the girl's heading for nursery-land.'

Stella pressed Momma's talon, 'Don't cry, Daphy.'

'Daphy! That let's me out of it'—Simon snorted with disgust at the word, thought of Laura and felt deeply relieved.

'I knew from the very beginning that I could give you such a wonderful time. I've got a little villa in Monte. Let's just drop everything, darling, and go tomorrow. Nigel could look after the club, couldn't you Nigel?'

The pianist flashed a neon grin. 'Off you go, girls, you have yourselves a ball.'

'There, it's all settled. I'll ring you when we've fixed the tickets and pick you up at that Borstal tomorrow. Nigel's a dream at fixing tickets. Momma must give him one great, big kiss.'

The pianist bore Daphne's pendulous hug with a stoical endurance.

'Now we can be really free,' Daphne pirouetted with unexpected agility and sitting down by Stella, oozed against her. The deep rolling voice was muted now; a kind of twittering. 'A man can't understand a woman like another woman. I know you had a yen for that little Armstrong, but it couldn't last, my pet, you're far too sensitive.' Daphne was trying to get the girl onto her lap. 'I don't exist for that pair now,' Simon was half pleased; one more drink and then home.

Madame stroked Stella's knee and pressed her lips against

the girl's ear. She shuddered slightly, drew away and looked at Simon.

'Blast the girl,' he muttered, 'she's coming up for the third and last time, and here I am on the bank watching.'

Daphne closed in again, 'It's sexually true, darling, you'll understand that when we're in Monte...'

Armstrong listened to the twittering and tried to ignore some still impregnable essence of his friend which stared through her eyes and questioned him. 'She doesn't want to regress to Mummy land, I'll have to try something. "Miss Clauberg?" '

She was too busy to hear him.

'It is true, I can make you feel that way far more than he could, because I'm a woman and know what we feel. He hasn't got anything that I can't give you...'

'Miss Clauberg,' Armstrong had used his 'large lecture hall' voice, and it did register. She turned towards him and grimaced, her teeth still red with lipstick.

'Oh God, don't tell me you're still here.'

'I'll be off in a moment, but my dear, where did you go to school?'

'What do you mean...poppet?' She tried to shape the usual drawl, but it was not effective.

'I couldn't help overhearing the conversation: "he hasn't got anything that I can't give you." Sorry, Miss Clauberg, but isn't your biology a trifle rusty?'

'Oh Stella, do tell the idiot to go away.'

Stella seemed to shake herself out of a dream as she got up and walked to the bar.

'On the contrary, it's just getting interesting, do go on, Simon.'

Speaking very dryly and distinctly he stalked across the room.

'I was merely pointing out the facts of life, your friend seems a little hazy. You see Daphne, both men and women do have tongues and fingers but there's a basic difference as regards the genital area. Women have a vagina, men have a penis.'

'No, don't do that, don't do it to me!' Daphne screamed as Stella snapped on the powerful neon light which was used only after hours when they counted the takings.

She seemed to melt in its glare and Simon felt some compassion, for Daphne was only a fat old woman now, and the urine trickling between her legs increased the sense of disintegration. But he went on with his speech as if it was a rite of exorcism.

'It's the difference that matters, like can only feed on like, feed and destroy, it's the opposition that makes more life, and that's what counts.'

Stella looked again at Daphne who lay flat on the sofa scrabbling at the cushions, then switched off the light. 'Let's go now.'

Nigel seemed sorry that the party was over, and started to vamp on the piano as they put their coats on.

'Blessed are the pure in heart,' Simon murmured to Stella as Nigel sang:

> 'I can't give you anything but love, baby,
> That's the only thing I've plenty of, baby,
> Dream a while, scheme a while,
> You're sure to find . . .'

'God knows what,' he thought, as holding Stella's hand he groped down the stairs of The Melting Pot, 'God knows what, but it appears that I am in the thick of it.'

10

'THAT's fresher,' Simon inhaled the loaded air of Soho, 'where to now? We're both in need of some refreshment.'

'My place ...?'

'Or mine, Laura very much wants to meet you.'

'I'm sure she does, but I've had enough tensions for one evening.'   ...

'Tensions?' He pretended not to understand. 'They're not a hobby of Laura's.'

Stella dug her nails into his hand. 'Don't be so crass, I want to talk to you, not Mr and Mrs Armstrong.'

'Right then, we'll split the difference and make it that drinking club, what do they call it, the ... Keller. Eight-thirty, it ought to be pretty empty now.'

They walked to this decayed and unfashionable club through a forest of strip-tease joints.

'No visible whores now,' said Simon. 'Apropos of the Street Offences Act an aunt of mine said she could never have believed a Conservative government would lay its hands upon the oldest profession.'

'You needn't sound so nostalgic. All that's happened is a field-day for voyeurs and the poor whores at the mercy of their ponces.'

Rows of pimps and doorkeepers peddled their erotic wares as Stella and Simon walked down Gnome Street towards New Creston Road. Like joints of meat, their substantial 'goodies' were displayed in photographs on either side of each seedy entrance. They resembled garish butchers' shops, but once inside, no solid nourishment was available; only 'near beer' and coca-cola at seven-and-six the knock, a brief vision of feminine nudity, then the executive from B'rum or Manchester would be excreted from the small red-lit room, lighter in pocket by a pound or two.

They turned the corner into New Creston Street, noticing the undercurrent of indefinable savagery in that area which some novelist had called 'the nastiest strip of land in

70

Western Europe.' No doubt it had something to do with drugs. A café roared as they passed its cargo of strangely-clad teenagers, and he imagined the sideslips of conversation in which pound notes were exchanged for small packages, whether of heroin or amphetamines. It had not been like this ten or twenty years ago when the painters Colquhoun and MacBride had drunk in the area with Tambimuttu and the poets George Barker, Dylan Thomas and John Heath Stubbs. MacClaren Ross had leaned foppishly against the bars and Louis MacNeice strayed down from The George; men and women whose witty ironic conversation had never bypassed the effort of swallowing beer.

'This savage undercurrent!' He nudged Stella as they passed a gaggle of five or six West Indians, straw-hatted, jeaned, voracious as gulls as they mobbed two short tarts from the Midlands who displayed on that corner of Soho a brash toughness only comparable to their vulnerability.

'Well, here's the Keller, shall we try it?'

'Your choice, love, but I wouldn't be sure it's all that empty.'

Simon entered the club which had been a favourite haunt of his twenties with some nostalgia but Stella was right. As he pushed through the beaded curtains he saw in a far corner the international figure of Nina Hamnett, her glass empty, waiting for a replenishing audience.

'Darlings.' Nina had endured a fall recently and half-rose from her seat of custom waving a battered crutch. 'Ahoy there, Armstrong!'

Once beautiful, in an original way, and the model of a number of distinguished artists, Nina was now tanned by alcohol. She was weather-beaten as her late father, the admiral, whom she still dearly loved and whose devotion had queered her pitch as far as a marriage was concerned, leaving her with a somewhat nebulous passion for sailors in general.

'Darlings, just get me a tiny drink and I'll tell you who I met this morning, you'll never guess—Archy Sullivan!'

'O God, she's off,' thought Simon, 'we must get out of here and quickly.'

Nina had long since been converted to the religion of

alcohol and had no words which were not in its praise. 'It was just like the old days, when Roy Campbell was around. Did I ever tell you how we met in Pedro's Club during the war and someone came in with four Polish seamen, such dears!'

'Yes,' Simon remarked, remembering his short war-time service as a gunner on a Polish merchant ship. 'I do remember, because it was I who introduced them to you.'

But Nina was away, there was not room in her monologue for a knife-blade.

'They were well loaded with cash and we stayed from three to six, drinking Vodka and Pernod. Roy was a bit bedraggled in those days; you know all the Fascist nonsense of his during the Spanish war. It reminded me of a day I spent in Paris with Modigliani . . .'

They both would have liked to question Nina about her liaison with the desolate master, but it was not possible. Once the conversation veered to an exploration of personality or conflict she whirled it back to the bottle and small talk like a skilled juggler.

'Yes, Modigliani did have black moods but not that day. Oh no, he was stinkers, mind you, but full of wit.'

Simon lit another cigarette and looked at her through the smoke fumes.

'You were happy, Nina?'

'Happy . . .?'

Stella nudged Simon. He must stop probing; for a terrible blank second the High Priestess of Alcohol had peered out of her cage of pickled meat into the bleak reality of a life without love, hate, relationship, only the consumption of distilled liquor.

'Just one more drink, darlings, if you can manage, and I reckon old Riccardo there could do with a snorter. Do you remember those Polish seamen, Riccardo?'

The barman, a brother of a famous wrestler, and slowly dying of cancer, nodded and smiled gratefully as he drained his whisky. 'Grazie.'

'But the Polish seamen,' Simon insisted. 'I introduced them to you, Nina, don't you remember?'

'God no, they were pukka sailors, Armstrong, Campbell

was with them.' Alcohol had shrivelled great swathes of Nina's memory and deprived her of any capacity for dialogue. Talking to her was like a switchback, up and down, with great yawning spaces between the leaps of language.

How far gone is she? thought Simon. He leant forward, 'Do they still come here, the Polish sailors?'

'Do they not, my old fruit,' he noticed that Riccardo's mouth had gaped open with astonishment, 'every second Friday for a jaunt with little Nina.'

Simon looked at the bronzed, aged woman supported by one crutch and a rabble of memories. The hound breath was close behind her now, and neither he nor Stella was surprised when some weeks later they read that she had fallen to her death from a fourth floor window.

It is always too late, he thought with interest and compassion when he was told how, bereft of the capacity to move swiftly from pub to pub, friends, or the illusion of amorous mariners, she had plunged through a crackle of chit-chat and alcohol into an area from which no statement, however incoherent, is customary.

'Deadybyes,' she would have said, but there was no smell of death on her when they left her in the drinking club, only the half-heroism of one who would neither surrender nor turn and face her pursuer.

The Swiss Pub really was empty. When he had got their drinks and had settled in a far corner, Simon looked at Stella, and again the sense of intimacy returned, of there being no skin between them, a completeness of meeting.

'Exactly how far gone were you with that woman at the Melting Pot?'

'I'll answer that, if you'll tell me how far you went with Chester.'

He grimaced at the memory.

'Our relationship splintered on the rock of homosexuality. It went swimmingly when I was living with Monique.'

'Spare me that one,' Stella grimaced at the mention of his mistress. 'Laura's quite enough to stomach.'

'You asked for the facts. I was saying that while John's 'husband'—Turkel I think his name was, yes—while Turkel was alive we made an excellent foursome. Two domestic couples and the talk was wonderful, then Turkel died of cancer and John, after quite a sharp bout of mourning, was fancy free.'

'He turned to you?'

'We turned to each other. Except for rock-climbing and the double bed Monique and I never had much in common so . . .'

'You left your woman at home, you went with Chester, you mopped up all you could of his genius. Really, Simon, when you want something, you are a selfish brute.'

'I could plead "poetic licence", but yes, it was something like that. When I look back on my past I realise I was very callous.'

'To put it mildly: but—you got 'very close' as they say and then—'embrassez-moi pour l'amour du grecque', or 'come up and see my etchings' . . . John wanted you to make love-hate to him, his special brand?'

'In Monte Carlo,' said Simon, 'at Daphne's villa.'

'So that's why you were so clever this evening!'

'Possibly, but I always wished he was a woman when I touched him. Bristles! that's what ended our . . .'

'Togetherness; did you think up that word, or was it Chester?'

'God knows,' Simon snapped, 'but now it's my turn for a question. Daphne hasn't a spark of aptitude, except for making money and seducing neurotic females, she's ugly, and she's splenetic, so how the hell did you let her get hold of you?'

'She wanted me and she made me feel wanted, not a vacuum any more.'

'Yes . . . I know that feeling.'

Stella rapped the table, 'I want to be wanted, indeed I do.'

'Then you'd have taken the morning plane to Gomorrah.'

'Can't you understand? It's not a question of mere people, I want to want and I want to be wanted.'

'But wasn't the bosom a deterrent, not to mention the urine?'

'I wasn't *me* any more, I was just a need,' she gripped his hand, 'but the next morning to wake up and find Daphne snoring beside me . . .!'

74

'Would that be intolerable?'

'Intolerable.'

'But you must have been with men, loved a man,' Simon stuttered, the old Lesbian phobia needling him. 'How could you have let that... female paw you?'

'I tell you I didn't *let* anything, whatever I was had been scrubbed out; Daphne was a mirage.'

'A substantial one, but—sorry to persist—the men in your life?'

Now Stella stammered, 'G-get me another drink, and I'll try to tell you. A strong one.' Her fingers trembled as she fiddled with her handbag.

'You should have got a fuller case history from Charles Abbott,' Stella swallowed half her drink. 'There haven't been any men, not in real love, not with their coming... inside me.'

'You mean that technically you're a virgin?'

'If you put it like that, but Simon, if I tell you what used to happen, you won't despise me, hate me?'

'Why should I? I told you my spiel and you took it.'

'I could take their,' she swallowed and gabbled on, 'things into my mouth and suck them, I could let them kiss me down there, but I couldn't let them come inside me.'

Simon was reasonably unshockable, unless someone touched a sore place. 'You meant cunnilingus was all right, and fellation, but not, dear Stella, copulation.' He shuddered at the rhyme but wanted to relieve her anxiety.

She seemed more relaxed. 'As you so cleverly put it. But it will be different now.' She looked at him steadily and questioning, but he bypassed her implied enquiry.

'Let's beg the difference for a moment. Sorry to be technical, and it's Abbott's job really, but we can't escape the levels.'

'You mean Freud's oral, anal and genital business?' said Stella, 'I've been through all that.'

'Yes. And Freud was right there, but they do have a deeper significance. First, you suck and bite, you take, and if you stay there you grow up into a kind of vampire, a parasite. Then you shit and give, savagely, that's where Chester is, the baby part of him, on the anal level, and 'anal giving', however magnificent its sublimation is always soaked in hatred. Then you fuck, I mean both take and give, hate serves love and you take and give; if you're lucky, with some discretion. The genital means a good deal more than happy copulation.'

Stella murmured,

> 'You, should hands explore a thigh,
> All the labouring heavens sigh,
> And I shall hear if we should kiss
> A contrapuntal serpent hiss . . .'

'I know you took an English Degree and we both like Yeats, but let's leave him out for a moment and be more earthy.'

'Isn't that Abbott's job?'

'It's anybody's ruddy job after your goings on in the Melting Pot.' Simon was surprised how angry he was at the memory of that huddle.

'Not to mention your goings on in the Lizard. I've heard that you slapped Chester's face and then kissed him. It's still talked about in these parts.'

'Sorry, I didn't mean to be pompous. But I do mean that you had lapsed to the breast level with that Daphne. You were Mummy's little girl again and that part of you wants to burrow right back and back into the womb . . .'

'There could be no end to that journey.'

'Perhaps . . . until they sound the trumpets. You didn't have the breast as a baby, you lacked security at that stage, so you could regress into a kind of free-for-all woman parading the town, and all the bloody bats would settle. Forgive the metaphors but all the parasites would be at you. And that,' he bent forward in the deserted bar and kissed her, 'that my love I would find unbearable.'

Stella looked at him steadily. 'You're quite right about me, but Simon Armstrong, I know your background and God help you if you don't realise you've also made a self-diagnosis.'

'I do know it.' He quoted Yeats reluctantly.

'And when we talked of growing up
Knew that we'd halved a soul,
And fell the one in t'other's arms
      That we might make it whole.'

'There,' she said, 'that's what I mean, we have halved a soul and that's why we can help complete each other. You have a wife, your daughter, your job, your reputation, but you're not whole and you never will be without me.'

'What follows?' Simon gazed at the impasse, the endless vistas of complexity that opened before him.

'This follows; you can help me to travel on further and I can help you. Can there be more than that for anyone? Only you and I can do this for each other. Do you know what you did for me back there, how you helped me, Simon, helped almost against your will because you want to be rid of me? I don't fit. But I've talked to you as to no one else tonight, even Charles Abbott and whether or not you think this is impulsive I do believe that there's a love which holds us both. That we and our circumstances have got to fit into that. You must come home with me.'

'If only it was as simple as that. Can't you see there's Laura.'

As if to dissolve his scruples he went quickly to the bar, ordered a pint and two double gins, drank his own gin at one gulp and then turned back to Stella.

She sat very still and musing, her head bent forward in deep concentration.

'Here you are.'

She blinked and looked up at him. 'Yes, there's Laura, but there could also be two other people; people who will turn to stone if they refuse the gift of each other.'

Simon drank half of his beer at one gulp. She was right of course, and his pulse quickened as he looked at her down-turned face, beautiful and brooding. But it was not a question of right and wrong, but of two rights in conflict. He did feel that he loved this woman, that some imaginative, forever unsatisfied energy of himself in her had found its nearest equivalent. But could he live without Laura or she without him, could he deny the years of experience,

77

shared and creative, which made their togetherness? What they had done together? It would be like cutting off great swathes of his memory, since what he remembered was mixed with her. And the understanding they had worked so long for, the intricate web of long shared feeling, the child. Two goods but the older had been tried and not found wanting. Talk could not solve the complexity of this situation. He must offer platitudes, and he turned to Stella who sat with her drink untasted.

'Drink up, darling, and listen, I do love my wife and I am beginning to love our adopted child. I think you know that I love you, but I am Simon Armstrong, I live in Windermere Road. I write poems, I have a wife and a child.'

'You talk as if life were an algebraic equation—we're not numbers, dead letters, we're living people and life doesn't follow rules; it's unpredictable.'

'Is it? I believe, I have come to believe, the hard way, that there are rules, even if they're invisible and can't be written down.'

'But for all your rules, we have this; if we don't take it, then what will become of us?'

'Become? For me marriage, poetry, work, for you I think more of Charles Abbott, more insight, love, marriage.'

'Christ!' snapped Stella, 'great thoughts, I want you—not a Wayside Pulpit.'

'Right then, I leave Laura and come over to you and bring my guilt with me. I'm not a deserter, but I would have deserted two people I love, who love and need me. What happens? The guilt pierces, then I start to blame you as the cause of it. Do you want that weight round your neck?'

' "Bear ye one another's burdens." But I get the point. All I ask is that you come back to me for this night. Say the fog's too bad and you've had to stay with a colleague, how will Laura know? Anyway, the fog is thick enough.'

Simon brought more drinks from the counter. 'I come home with you, we make love, it is, as you say, what a certain fate intends for us. Then tomorrow when the fog has lifted, more love-making, but the bill is presented. "Öd

78

und leer das Meer," "Barren and empty the sea," I leave you. Let's say we learn to love each other body and soul, the soul may manage, but our bodies will be apart, yours in Herbert Grove, mine in Windermere Drive or at the Welsh Cottage . . .'

'I can take it.'

'Even if you could it wouldn't work. Lies aren't viable with people you know well. Laura would know what had happened—then the usual domestic erosion.'

'You certainly do play for safety.'

'I play as well as I can. Moreover, love, I do believe that you've moved on already, that you can't be harmed again, not in the same way.'

'As for myself,' Simon listened to a street singer as they walked out into the fog—'I know where I'm going and I know who's going with me, I know whom I love, but the devil knows . . .'

The Devil knows, he thought, as he whistled up Stella's taxi.

11

LAURA had a slight cold and was asleep when he came home, so Simon slept in the spare room, Stella weaving in and out of his dreams.

'Ouch!' he was jerked awake by a sharp stab in the ribs.

'Boo.' Rhoda was grinning about six inches from his face, her eyes barbed with affection and mischief.

This, he thought, rubbing his side and smiling, is reality.

'What are you up to, you monkey, it can't be six o'clock.'

''Tis, 'tis, 'tis,' she pirouetted round the room. 'I wanted to wake you then, but Mummy stopped me, it's half past nine and you're a slowcoach, and breakfast's ready and remember you promised . . .'

'Promised what?'

'Oh Lord,' he thought, 'the vulnerability of children!'

Rhoda had stopped in her tracks and her face was a diagram of shock and disappointment.

'Don't take on love, I haven't woken up yet, tell Dad what he promised and you shall have it.'

She gave a brisk leap on to his stomach and began to bounce. 'To take me to the park, Mummy told me.'

'Then the park it will be.'

Rhoda nuzzled her face into his neck, then sniffed suspiciously. 'You smell funny.'

'And you're a little bloodhound.' He realised guiltily that she'd picked up Stella's scent, and got up to wash in the handbasin.

'What's a bloodhound?'

'It's a great big dog with long, droopy ears and it follows smells and it finds people.'

The thread had broken, Rhoda was on her knees sniffing round the carpet, she was a bloodhound.

'Ready, darling,' Laura came over and kissed him, 'it's a gorgeous day, frosty, I think I'll come too.'

'Good,' said the child firmly, 'Let's go! Come on, Dad, hurry.'

Armstrong dressed, scrambled through his breakfast, noticing with satisfaction that the proofs of a new book had arrived and in less than an hour they were at the park.

Rhoda was out of the car before he had switched off the engine and raced towards the statue of Alderman Batley; it had many convenient projections and its ascent was part of her 'park routine'.

'At least the thing has some value,' said Laura, as their daughter climbed neatly towards the bald stone pate of the donor of the park.

The statue was quite something. The civic authority had been advised by the University Art Department to commission John Chester. But his price was 4,000 guineas 'and that,' said the mayor to his assembled council, 'is a hell of a lot of money.' Alderman Barker solved the situation. 'What about one of our chaps? I believe old Sam Moult would do us a very decent job for a couple of hundred.'

The stonemason had done them proud. Alderman Batley's left hand rested on the exact replica of a Spinning Jenny, his right on the laurel-crowned head of a female figure, into whose modest drapes Sam Moult had chiselled the word 'chastity'. There was a stone rose in the alderman's button-hole, and Simon noted that Rhoda was using it as a foothold while her hand gripped his pate.

'Did you meet Chester?'

'I certainly did and it was bloody awful—I shan't go to that snake-pit again.'

'Not even with Stella?' she brushed a streak of powder from his lapel; 'really darling, it seems to have been quite a party.'

Simon flushed and the words came out involuntarily. 'Damn it, didn't I tell you that it was bloody awful.'

'She's certainly bitten you, but you needn't take it out of me. How is the woman?'

'Mind your bloody . . .' he noticed Rhoda had made the summit and was racing back to them and checked himself. 'She was *comme ci, comme ça*. I'll tell you later, at the moment it's sticklebacks.'

'I always suspect the worst when you put on that ghastly French accent. Still, as you say, sticklebacks, but remember

I do exist, my darling.'

The pond was not iced over but shone with the radiance of congealing water. It poised between liquid and solid. The birds it offered to a rinsed sky, town-habitué mallards, who liked life easy, coots, moorhen and a pair of crested grebes, dipped and surfaced with exceptional vigour, as if they were storing up life against a coming ice-age.

It wasn't the time for fishing but Rhoda plunged her net into the transparent water. 'Got him,' she scooped a small newt from its muddy hideout. 'Where's the jar, mum?'

The thin green slip of sleepy life jerked in the meshes.

'Poor little soul, let's put it back, darling. It will die if we don't. It wants to hibernate.'

'Mummy, what's hibernate?'

'They get under the mud and sleep right through the cold winter. Put her back and let her go to sleep again.'

'How do you know it's a she, aren't there he's and don't they get caught too?'

'There are and they do,' Simon turned from them and was apparently addressing a fir tree, 'some of them want to sleep but they cannot, "Macbeth doth murder sleep and therefore Cawdor shall sleep no more." '

'What's murder?'

'Killing someone,' said Laura sharply, as she glanced at her husband. 'Now, put it back, love, or it will catch cold and die.'

Rather sadly, Rhoda relinquished her prey.

'Now swings,' said Simon, 'come on, Rhoda.'

'Higher, higher, higher,' he enjoyed her delight in exciting movement as he pushed the child skyward. His own mother had been terrified of freedom and had kept him on leading strings. He was redressing the balance, and enjoying vicariously a pleasure which as a child he had never been allowed.

'Watch it, love, she's not all that clever,' Laura looked anxious, 'She's almost level with the crossbar.'

Rhoda swooped back towards him, 'Again,' she crowed, 'Just one more.'

As Simon bent back for another thrust, he saw the spire of a church which bore his name. It was golden in the frosty mist. 'She walks in beauty like the night.'

'Christ! Now you've done it!'

Laura raced towards their child who had shot out of her swing from his last thrust, somersaulted, then come to rest on the hard trodden grass. She gathered up Rhoda, who— 'Thank God', he thought, 'she can't be too badly injured'— began to bawl loudly.

'Do you want to kill the girl?'

He moistened his handkerchief with spittle and wiped the grit from her gashed forehead. 'Are you all right, pet, are you?'

She opened her arms and hugged him tearfully. 'I'm sorry, I didn't mean to let go, don't be angry.'

'Of course you didn't, my pet, it was my fault, I pushed too hard.'

'You certainly did,' murmured Laura, as with their dazed child pig-a-back on his shoulders, they walked to the car.

'What do you mean?' Simon saw the spire again, fading in the December twilight. 'I was only playing with her.'

'My God you were! That last shove of yours would have dislodged an elephant. You'd better watch your day-dreams or . . .'

'Or bloody what?' He was surprised at his bitter irritation.

'There you go again, that wasn't necessary.'

'For God's sake woman, don't hint, tell me what you mean.' He felt the child move on his shoulders.

'I mean that when you pushed Rhoda that last time, I saw your face; you were miles away, and I want to know what happened last night.'

'Sweet FA and you know it or I wouldn't have been at home this morning, nor heard you snoring when I came in.'

'I don't snore.'

'Like a pig,' said Professor Armstrong, but the quarrel was cut short by his burden. It began to sob.

'My head hurts, and you're quarrelling, and I'm not comfy and we haven't got any fishes.'

They looked at each other guiltily. 'It's all right, nearly there now.'

They passed the smug stone mask of Alderman Batley. 'All the same,' he thought, 'I bet you made a damn sight better husband and father than I am.'

Laura answered his thought. 'There's some virtue in being short-sighted, but we're not short-sighted, Simon, and you can't wriggle out of it ...'

'Hold it. Rhoda!'

'Rhoda will have to take it. I'm saying there are rules and, much as I love you, if I'm to be with you then you must keep them.'

'And that,' he said, 'is the exact conclusion I came to last night with Stella.'

'You mean ...?'

'I mean that you and Rhoda are all that matters. I shan't see the woman again and no more jaunts to that foul Melting Pot.'

He felt Rhoda relax and lean forward, nuzzling her face into his neck.

Laura had a cold. He was right about the snoring and went to sleep again in the spare room after a bout of television.

As he slept he saw that his room was changing colour from pink to red until it deepened into a dark crimson. From some remote corner he could see his own bed but it was empty. Who was it coming? The door was shut but he could hear slow, heavy footsteps on the staircase. Blind hands fumbled on the door, then the handle turned, the door opened and it was present. The creature framed in the doorway was undoubtedly related to himself under the thick red pelt that covered its stooping body. He had dreamt before of those enormous hands with their claw-nails, the wolf muzzle that lolled forward from a muff of pricking fur. But this time it was closer, more real than ever before. He could hear the snuffing sound of its questing breath, as blind, it shuffled forward towards the bed where his wife slept. It grasped the bedposts, slid round and took hold of the pillows, squeezing and throttling. Nothing. He could hear its sharp grunt of frustrated savagery as it dropped the empty pillows. Then he heard a thin gasp. Laura was standing at the door looking for him. He tried to cry out a warning but his throat was stopped and dry; no sound came. The werewolf turned softly towards Laura at the door, slid towards the left wall and groped towards her silently, its great hands feeling its way. 'Run! For God's sake get out of it,' he tried to shout but again his parched throat could make no sound. Laura walked forward as if in a dream and then the creature was on her, grasping, its great head bent towards her throat and biting downwards. At last he could hear his own voice, panicked and screaming.

Laura was beside him. 'It's all right . . . darling, I'm with you, it's only a nightmare.'

Simon hugged his wife to him and sobbed, 'It was going to kill you.'

'It's a nightmare like you used to have when we first got married; The Melting Pot must have brought it back again.'

He touched his wife's throat and neck as he jerked from his dream. They were cool and unmarked. He looked at his hands and there was no blood on them. He relaxed with relief and kissed Laura very tenderly.

His wife got into bed beside him, 'Goodnight, my darling, goodnight.'

12

THE RICH and egocentric architect who owned most of the valley in which Simon and Laura rented their Welsh cottage would sell none of his land and would only let his cottages to recommended tenants of some artistic or intellectual standing. Consequently, his valley was not disfigured by modernist villas, caravan sites, or transistor radios. The local pub was frequented by a more bizarre and colourful brainstorm of intellectuals than the whole of Chelsea.

It was Easter and almost a year after the incident in the Melting Pot. Simon and Laura had engaged a Welsh girl to look after Rhoda in the cottage and were sitting in The Spinning Wheel. They were deafened by the roar of artistic chatter and amused by the diversity of fishing jerseys, capes and sombreros which were a perpetual source of interest to the few locals who braved the single bar. It milled over artistic and intellectual problems like a computer.

'At it again.' Charles stood grinning down at them, clad in knickerbockers and a climbing jacket. 'I've come up from town in seven hours and I well deserve a large pint of bitter.'

'Lovely to see you, Charles, and you're driving again?'

'With a crippling insurance.'

Laura moved up on the three-seater commode of ancient black Welsh oak to make room for him while Simon got some more beer.

'How long can you stay?'

'As long as possible, and that means until I get a desperate telegram from the clinic. Things have been rather hectic lately as I've had a suicide, successful—if that's the word—on my hands. You know how I loathe them; but this might have been a case for old Power and a lobotomy.'

'It must have been one hell of a worry. But on the credit side, the weather's perfect and should remain so for a good few days.'

'The credit side . . .' not for the first time, Laura wondered at her husband's curious local callousness; he had made no response to Abbott's remark of suicide.

'Well, that's something,' said Charles, 'I'm itching to do a bit of climbing. But you'll have to lead, Simon, I'm in foul training.'

Simon went to the gents. During his absence Charles looked closely at Laura.

'I thought the air here was good for you. But you've lost weight that you can ill spare, and you're too pale.'

'I'm so glad you've come, Charles, you always bring good luck and I need it! No, I'm not very well, bronchial trouble as usual, but the antibiotics keep that at bay, thank Heaven. No I'm worried, perhaps I can tell you later . . .'

Simon was coming back. Laura continued in a slightly raised voice, 'Rhoda's wonderful, in fine form . . .'

'I imagine that she is,' said Charles, 'it's you I'm worried about.'

'So am I.' Simon's voice was strained.

'You shouldn't really have come out tonight, only it seemed a pity to refuse Myfamwy's offer of a baby-sitting. If you're not better tomorrow we'll stay in with you.'

He turned to Charles. 'I've done quite a bit of scrambling during the last few days and if Laura's OK, I'd be delighted to lead you up the Ridge Route.'

'Excellent; long, beautiful but not too hard. But this parrot house! Let's get a few bottles of beer and go to your place.'

They followed each other up the narrow twisting road to Bryn Fawr.

'One doesn't see the stars in London,' said Charles, as he got out and stretched in front of the cottage.

'In town, it's just a pink or grey fuzz. As for the air, one doesn't realise what muck one has been absorbing till one inhales this. Here we are then. Laura love, can you knock us up something to eat? I'm famished.'

While Laura was cooking, Simon and Charles walked towards Cnicht, the symmetrical little mountain that hovered over their cottage like a benevolent god. A new moon swam over its overshadowing shoulder and they could hear the quiet cropping of sheep, the hoot of an owl, the speech of running water.

'Tomorrow the Ridge Route,' said Charles. 'Will it be popular with Laura? Perhaps she could walk up to the climb with Rhoda and take her painting things?'

'Laura? She will do, as you well know, exactly what she wants. That, I expect, will be a walk round Cnicht with Rhoda. Anyway, Rhoda might find the long thrash up to Llwedd a little trying. Particularly as she's a great one for peering into pools and collecting plants for our rock-garden.'

'Something else they share. Well, let's get off at a reasonable hour tomorrow. As I said, I'm in shocking training. But it's marvellous to be seeing Pen-y-Pass again and those twin peaks, not to mention the summit of Snowdon. Only one carping bit of criticism, my dear Simon. I hate saying it, but Laura is not looking very well, and she's smoking a damn sight too much, chain smoking; can't you and I do a little tactful discouragement?'

'I know all about it,' Simon replied, 'so does Laura, in fact she was told to keep off smoking when we went to the Chest Clinic. "Lay off or you'll become a chronic bronchitic," she was told. Well, she did lay off for a few weeks, but now she's at her twenty or thirty again and whatever I say makes no difference. Incidentally, I must call in at the chemist and pick up her antibiotics tomorrow. They do keep bronchitis at bay.'

'Professor Armstrong, it is, Armstrong the poet, and, if my eyes don't deceive me, Dr Abbott, the brains. This is a great pleasure.'

When he had pocketed his shilling, Glyn Owen grasped their hands. By some ancient but irrefutable title deed, the hill farmer owned half a mile of lucrative parking space near the hub of Snowdon. He did remarkably well from the current enthusiasm for mountains but had little time for the newer, brasher recruits and was glad to see his old clients.

Abbott glanced at the crammed car park and slapped his friend's shoulder. 'No need to ask how you're doing, Owen the Park. When are you going to put up the prices?'

88

'Up they are already, Abbott bach, but how long is it since you first came here, thirty years? We were lads then. I haven't the heart to charge you.'

Presided over by a large man wearing a commando beret, a dozen youths slumped out of a minibus. There was a shrill blast on his whistle and they trailed off sadly behind him.

'Where the hell do they go?' asked Simon.

'Up to the lake for some good Welsh air, it's cheap at the price; that lot will be doing the Horse Shoe.'

'Doing's the word,' said Abbott, 'there should be a bit of hard snow and ice on the Crib Coch ridge, and their Führer didn't have an ice axe.'

'It will be thawing now,' said Owen, 'the first part will be like a bog and I wouldn't trust my poor cattle on it. But I'm told the Horse Shoe is more slippery with orange peel than ice, man.'

'Well, we're off to Llwedd, see you back at the pub then.'

'Indeed yes, but I would take an axe, there may be some icy patches on the mountain.'

Simon took his ice axe from the car and threaded it through the loops of his rucksack. Llwedd might have some slippery bits and he had a healthy respect for the crag. Although it offered the longest climbs in Wales, and had routes of some thousand feet in length, it had fallen from popularity since their climbing heyday and was rarely visited. It was too difficult for beginners and did not have enough technical problems and aerobatics for the modern expert.

'A lot of these chaps,' said Abbott, as two bearded youths strode past them, clinking with pitons and karabinas, 'aren't particularly fond of mountains. They do all the top grade climbs that are near the road, do them in about three years, then stop. It's mainly one-upmanship.'

'They can't rise a foot in the Pass without an audience, but praise the Lord for human solidarity, it leaves this to us . . .'

Llwedd's enormous twin peaks were rarely touched with the sun, and seemed to grow larger as they toiled towards them. There were streaks of ice here and there but not enough to make serious difficulty. Simon and Charles had climbed the cliff for many years and now pointed out to each other every detail, the Horned Crag, the Quartz Babe, the Great Terrace, the Central Gulley.

Years ago they might have considered the Ridge Route an energetic scramble. Although a good seven hundred feet in length and pleasantly varied—there were chimneys, walls, a splendid traverse leading on to an airy knife-edge arête— it was described by the guide book as 'pleasant and domestic'.

'It will be a little less domestic today,' Simon thought. As he undid the rope by the twin quartz streaks that marked the start of the climb, he noticed long sheets of ice on the moderately steep glacis. It would be necessary to pick one's way between them until they reached the steeper rocks which would probably be clear.

' "Climbing!" as they say in the Ever Upward Schools.' He took a last tug at his waist knot and stepped delicately on to the sloping rocks, feeling the usual prickling of fear and excitement which always marked the start of a climb. He was glad of his axe and chipped an occasional foothold as he worked up to the first wall.

'I'll put a runner on here, watch the rope for a change,' Simon shouted affectionately to Abbott who, some eighty feet below, was having a spirited conversation with an invisible companion. 'I said—watch the rope, I'm putting on a runner.' Charles nodded and putting the loose rope round his waist began to pay out carefully. Simon slipped his rope through the steel clip he had clicked on to a sling hung over a spike of rock and thus protected, started up the short steep wall. He knew it by heart, in every sense; brushed a film of powder snow from one foothold, jammed his right hand into a slim crack, placed one foot on the foothold, the other back against the side wall and with a couple of well-placed thrusts was up and over. As he drew in the rope he thought of Rhoda. Scrambling about near the cottage she had seemed remarkably agile and sure-footed. If it was a decent day tomorrow, he would try her on the Milestone Buttress.

'Here you are, Charles.'

'Very nice, too, but I envy your condition, I'm puffing like a grampus.'

The next pitch was excellent. You stepped delicately down and round a great prow of granite on to a small plate of rock on the edge of all things. It seemed at first sight to be a blank end, but running up leftwards was a shallow groove worn smooth by many boots and venerable backsides. The rock was perfectly dry and touched by light frosty sunlight. He wished Laura was with them but she was probably still in bed, coughing. 'Oh hell, I've forgotten her antibiotics, must pick them up before we go to the pub. If only human problems were as straightforward as this!' Using small pockmarks on the right wall to steady himself, he crawled up the forty-foot groove, and was on to the grassy platform that ended the pitch, and felt for a small spike of rock that pushed through grass and heather.

Charles was soon beside him and they looked at the steep open chimney that was the crux of the climb. Two narrow cracks gave some hand and foothold but they were remarkably smooth at one point and it was necessary to use an incut nick on the right wall and a sloping foothold high up to the left of the chimney.

'Well, here goes and watch out, I'll be putting on a runner.' He balanced up the crux. 'What in Hell will they be up to next!'

'What's up?'

'A kitchen poker. Some humorist has jammed it across the twin cracks so that it cuts out the interesting bit. Firm too, I shan't need a runner.'

'I'll take a good sharp stone,' Charles grunted. 'This is blasphemy!'

Simon was soon up and tied onto a large rock bollard, took in the rope. 'OK Charles, I'll keep a good hold while you knock out the ironmongery.'

There were a few sharp ringing blows; then he saw the poker curve out into space and plunge towards the scree five hundred feet below. 'Whoever put that in will have a nice surprise when he has another go at the Ridge Route. It's one thing in the Dolomites when the rock's as loose as a slag heap. Well, now the traverse; it's my favourite place.

You'd better carry on leading.

Abbott quickly followed him to the summit, and they saw and heard the approaching Ever Upwards group. Except for the leader, who was bouncing gaily ahead, giving an occasional glance at his wrist-compass, it was a sombre party.

'Poor sods,' said Charles, 'do you know that some firms insist on their juniors spending a part of their holidays on these jaunts? It's supposed to build character. But what's he doing with that thing? A blind Pekinese could find his way round the Horseshoe in this weather.'

'Cutting a dash and putting his merry men off the mountains for life.'

The Führer had taken his bearings and stood, one arm outstretched, on a large boulder. He took the whistle that hung from a pipeclayed lanyard and blew a piercing blast. 'Come on, my lucky lads, four hours is the schedule and four hours it's going to be. Put some beef into it.'

Under enormous haversacks, the 'lucky lads' staggered onwards.

'Good day to you, gentlemen! Trust you enjoyed the Ridge Route. You may have noticed that I've ironed out one little problem.'

'You mean the chimney?'

'Yes, just an old kitchen poker but I think you'll agree it's improved the climb. Sorry, Gerald, but no smoking in the ranks.'

Sadly, a fat bespectacled youth replaced his Woodbine.

'Am I to take it, young man, that you were responsible for that bit of ironmongery?'

'Ironmongery, ha ha, I don't know about that, sir, but you must admit it makes the climb more rational.'

Very deliberately, Abbott lit a cheroot and inhaled deeply.

'I don't know what the devil you mean by 'more rational', but your kitchen instrument is now resting happily on the scree some thousand feet beneath us.'

'Am I to take it, sir . . .?'

'I removed your poker because I have a wholesome regard for Welsh rock and have no wish to see a fine climb turned into a circus.'

The Führer looked both hurt and spiteful but the Horse-shoe was listed four hours. He looked at his watch and compass, bawled 'Sixteen hundred hours' and followed by a desolate string of apprentices bounced forward.

Simon and Charles sauntered down from the mountain slowly so as to reach the pub at opening time. The Vernon Arms of Nant Peris had resisted change. There were the same china cats, the same prints, the same chilly, smoky little fire, the hard wooden pews and oak tables. On the left wall Queen Victoria continued to melt into tears as she pinned a medal on a blinded hero of the Crimea.

One of the two sisters who ran the Arms shuffled out of her dark, simmering kitchen. Clad in black drapery and with her hair dangling like weed over her grey brow, she greeted them with what for her was enthusiasm.

'So here you are again, Mr Armstrong bach, and Dr Abbott, now what will it be for you, two pints of my special mild?'

Abbott shuddered slightly at the mention of her 'special'.

'No, thank you, Blodwen dear, two pint bottles of Double Diamond in mugs. Don't suppose you have any cigarettes?'

'No indeed, the licence, Mr Charles bach, desperately expensive it is.'

'Thanks, love, will you have something?'

'No thank you. I've just had a cup of tea, and how is Mrs Armstrong?'

'Well, she's coughing a bit.'

'But you two must be fresh from the mountains. At your age too, going against nature it is.'

'On the contrary, it's to your mountains that we owe our remarkable youth and celerity. How are you and your sister doing?'

'Very nicely, thank you dear, but small thanks to Lord Dunhavon.'

Simon remembered that the peer who owned the Valley had wanted to enlarge the pub and get a little more from the weekend climbers than empty tins and an increase in the rat population.

'Yes, I heard he wanted to make changes. Pity, your house has character.' He glanced at the enormous yellowing

93

photograph of four climbers in the Great Gully of Craig-y-Isfar. One would not look upon its like again. It had been taken by a box camera and every detail of the rock and stalwart bewhiskered mountaineers stood out with clarity. The leader was starting on the final crack and had raised a warning finger, 'Silence while the leader advances', thought Simon, 'the picture is nearly audible.'

'You climbed well today,' said Abbott, 'Still worried about Laura?'

'Obviously . . . I've forgotten her antibiotics.'

'Get them first thing in the morning; she seems basically sound and her cough is partly psychosomatic. Don't nag her. By the way, Stella Johnson is doing well. It must be a year since you saw her.'

'Quite so, and she is doing . . . well?'

'Yes, thanks to you and the Gods. One of my more success-ful patients. I was at a dead end but you certainly got her going with your evening at the Melting Pot. She could talk freely after that for the first time. And you were right not to answer the telephone though I imagine you were pretty caught up with her yourself at the time, and it can't have been easy for you—or Laura.'

'It wasn't. But what do you mean by "successful"?'

'I mean that after a brisk but not too serious attempt at suicide—barbiturates, she gave up the club, began to make a new set of friends and now she's engaged to be married. Hold hard, Simon! That's interesting!'

Armstrong had jerked his glass and beer swilled over the table.

'So it's still needling you?' Abbott looked searchingly at his friend, while Megan mopped the table muttering, 'What did I say? Climbing, when you are fifty years of age! It's against nature.'

'Sorry Charles, I never expected this news—or my re-action; it felt like a kick in the guts. Obviously I'm still involved.'

'Yes, but with what?' queried Abbott, noticing how his friend's hands were shaking. 'You'd better talk about it and you'd better face it; Stella is engaged to Roger Harton.'

'You mean Lord Saltmarch's son, the chap who drifted

around in a black cape with hair down to his backside?'

'Of course not, didn't I say I was pleased with Stella. Harton is a relative, in fact I think he's staying at the castle now and with Stella, but he's no hippy, he's a very sensible young man. Bright too; he's in your racket, got a Fellowship in English at Cambridge.'

'Is it what you might call a going concern?'

'I'm not a clairvoyant, but yes, I'd say they have a good chance of making a successful marriage. So let her out of your fantasies.'

'I thought I had done, but apparently she's still inside me; that's why I've been nagging at Laura.'

'Laura has to be a blend of a policewoman, an ever-open milkbar and your late lamented mother; that's quite something to cope with.'

'What can I do?'

'Meet Stella again, she's over here now. As a matter of fact I'd hoped you'd meet, see her as a real person, not your fantasy of a White Goddess. She doesn't need that any more.'

'Do you say she's here?'

'Yes and . . . six forty-five! It's a hundred to one they'll be in the Pitchfork by now. Come on, let's be off.'

The Pitchfork was on the estate of the same architect. He had a passion for landscape gardening on the grand scale. Near the pub a ruined tower was posed decoratively on a small hilltop and they parked the car by a large damp grotto. Its small waterfall had been deftly glided into a marble ewer and the attendant deity of the grove, a somewhat matronly marble Diana, smiled into its pale water.

The lights were going on in the cottages of Fanshaw's recommended tenants. Abbott groaned as they entered the packed bar. The locals were still struggling to play darts but it was not easy under the shattering word power of Chelsea and Hampstead.

William Coleridge, a television producer of some fame, and his attendant admirers were the main obstacle. Charles slid past him and weaved back with two pints of bitter. 'Where the hell are they?'

'If they're here and their rapport is ticking over as you

suggest, let's try the side bar.'

They edged past the dart players and went into the chilly room which took the Fork's spillover.

'Charles!' Stella surfaced from its far corner, and kissed Abbott, 'Simon too, come and meet Rob before we're suffocated.'

'Good evening, sir, delighted to meet you.'

Abbott was right, thought Simon, he is a pleasant youth, but I wish he didn't treat me like a stuffed Tennyson.

'I hope this isn't corny, sir, but I do know your work and greatly admire it, both the poems and the criticism. Stella's told me a lot about you.'

'Not too much, I trust,' Abbott grinned from behind his cheroot. 'Poets are a pretty nasty bunch when you get through their word barrage. Mary Shelley, for instance; she couldn't have created her monster if she hadn't the bard for a model. Ineffectual angel!'

'Don't exaggerate, Charles,' Stella sounded petulant, 'Shelley was Shelley.'

'I wasn't suggesting he was a hyena or a tomcat, merely somewhat lacking in charity. Traipsing round Europe leaving dead babies in his wake.'

'The intellect of man is forced to choose, perfection of the life or of the work,' quoted Harton, self-consciously.

'Oh God,' thought Simon, 'he is "instant literature"!'

'You mean he was too busy to be human?' asked Stella.

'Like so many others, Byron, for instance, Wordsworth, Marlowe; aren't you lucky to have a nice tame don for your future husband?'

'Not too tame, I trust,' Simon looked at Stella in her scarlet coat, 'anyway you have got a wild novelist on your hands.'

'Congratulations, Stella,' Abbott raised his glass, 'I hear your novel is being published.'

'Thanks to you and Rob or I wouldn't have got a word down.'

'I believe there's a kind of celebration on the day of publication. Do you have to make a speech?'

'I don't know about that, but I do know what I'm going to wear and it will be quite something.'

Abbott's right, thought Simon, she is a formidable creature. I wouldn't like to be her squire at the publication lunch, not my line. He turned to Robert.

'You're going to have a double role, husband and impresario.'

'Take no notice of Armstrong's wisecracks.' Abbott had noticed that Robert flushed although he did not reply to Simon. 'Be a good chap, make a raid on the bar; it will be two pints of Tankard for me and my tiresome friend.' Simon felt Abbott's boot ram against his outstretched leg.

'And a large gin for me, darling; I'll come and help you carry.'

'Why that crack?' Charles asked as Robert and Stella elbowed to the bar. 'It wasn't helpful.'

'It just came out; I was talking to myself really.'

'Not to mention trying to trip up Robert. You do realise you stretched out your leg in the very best position to make him tumble?'

'No, I didn't realise it.' Slowly Simon felt it sluicing through him, an intense jealousy.

'Then you and I have got some work to do.

'Maybe, but this meeting was a masterstroke. I really feel I'm getting Stella into focus.'

'Possibly, but it doesn't tally with your crack, not to mention your attempt to trip up Robert. It was quite intentional although you may not realise it.'

'A pint for you and a pint for Simon,' Stella and Robert had penetrated the barrage with remarkable speed and were back at the table. 'Have you finished your *Cult of the Vampire?*'

'Diffi*cult*.' Simon noticed Robert winking at Stella, 'It was a seedy pun but the old boy must be humoured.'

'I'm a short-distance writer, but this book has got hold of me and is getting longer and longer.' He looked at Charles. 'The vampire complex isn't merely a folie-à-deux, of that I'm certain. No. "My name is Legion, for we are many".'

Robert and Stella looked at him closely. Charles leant forward. 'What do you mean?'

'I mean when someone's bitten by a vampire, infected either literally or in a psychological sense by a lethal

97

parasite, then he is infected, recruited...' he stared into the thickening twilight, 'permanently recruited into the legion of the lost. It doesn't matter whether the source of infection is dead and done with. He is contaminated.'

'But there are rites of exorcism,' said Abbott.

'Analysis?—but it must be an ordeal. No intellectual game, but as painful as that stake the stories say must be driven through the heart of the vampire.'

'When the stake drives home,' Abbott sucked thoughtfully at his cigar, 'then the old creature who appears so young is old again—perhaps no more than a handful of living dust. That is the stake through the heart. It is not easy to give up an ingrown childhood, be weaned from others' "blood" and know one is alone and dying.'

'But better,' Simon's knuckles clenched white round his pint mug, 'better than preserving a fool's paradise. If one can live alone then one is not really alone, one is sustained.'

Stella murmured, ' "Lo, I am with you always even unto the end of the world." '

Once more Simon was delighted at her understanding.

'Precisely—it is the vampire, the one who dares not be alone who is in solitude. He is unsustained because he has declined real sustenance.'

'I'm not sure what you meant by that last little speech,' said Charles, when they had said goodbye to Robert and Stella and had turned up the road to the cottage.

'Why should you? I'm not. Perhaps water, "living water" is more sustaining than blood. Perhaps we must give up blood for water. But let's stop being metaphorical. One good point, this meeting has shown me that Stella's free. I'm fond of you Charles, you've helped by this meeting.'

'Then life should be easier for you and your marriage should work smoother as well. I gather you've given Laura a fairly hectic time, what with Rhoda being with you, and your work on *The Cult of the Vampire*.'

'You're right. I've been damned unpredictable. But the point I was trying to make in the pub was that obsession can continue when the person who started it off has gone; is no longer cared for. I'm not obsessed by Stella any more, but I'm still obsessed, haunted.'

'Oh Christ!' said Abbott, 'I'll have to put your case to my schizoids. You mean that Stella was only a precipitate or rather the thin edge of the wedge that opened you to this vampire obsession.'

'Yes, this meeting may have exorcised a person, but the person was only a mask and now I've got to face what's underneath.'

'Isn't it your Muse? Isn't poetry your form of exorcism?'

'Let's hope it's that. But it's been pretty bad recently.'

'You mean your black-outs? Laura has told me about them and she's been really frightened.'

'So am I. Something seems to take over, but thank God I haven't hurt her, not physically.'

'But you might and she knows it. You've been blacking out after booze, then gabbling about some imaginary creature you call Stella though she's not Stella or the BVM. More likely the bride of Dracula. Then you rail in your drink at your wife because she's not this fantasy and stops you getting at her. Look, I'm worried about Laura now.'

Simon was also deeply worried.

Together they hurried down the grass track to the cottage and as they reached the last curve could hear a paroxysm of coughing. It seemed to come from the depth of the earth and fill the night, blotting out all its tiny noises.

'That sounds bloody awful,' Charles muttered, 'come on, man, run.'

Her bedclothes scattered in tangles about the room, flushed with high fever and kneeling on the bed, her head thrust downwards into the mattress, Laura was fighting for life against the sputum in which she was drowning. As they entered, the wave of bronchitis flooded over her again. Her face almost black with the convulsive effort, she strove desperately for breath against the liquid that seeped up from the marsh of her small racked steaming body; fought and fought again, gasping until at last the bout receded; and she turned her small exhausted face towards Charles, 'Thank God you've come. I need a doctor.'

Abbott knelt by the bed and took her hand feeling upwards for the pulse.

'We're here, darling, it will be all right now. We're both

here.' She looked round the room in unseeing delirium, looked through and away from her husband. 'No. Keep Simon away from me,' her delirious voice sagged through a net of spittle, 'he wants to kill me, keep him away, away.'

'Yes, love. Simon, are there no antibiotics, she's in a raging fever.'

Trembling, Simon opened the door of the bedside table. One oval tablet was in the little glass bottle. He handed it to Abbott.

'That's not enough, man. For God's sake get some more. The chemists are shut. Go over to Dr O'Neill, the other side of the Moelwyns.'

Simon snatched a torch and started up the grassy trod which led to the col between Cnicht and the Moelwynians, then down to Blaenau. There was a village on the far side, deserted when the slate trade was broken. Dr O'Neill's house was near a desolate, roofless chapel, the last house before the track plunged down to the village. The road up was perfectly feasible even under snow for the doctor's formidable jeep, but O'Neill had retreated from telephones after decades at their beck and call, and Simon knew to his cost that the road to Dinas Confree was too rough and steep for his Hillman. He paced past the barking dogs of Ben's farm and was on to the rough steep path that led to Blaenau. For a while the moon was hidden by the great Moor's head of the mountain and it was very dark. He discarded the muted violence of the past weeks, blotted out Laura's feverish voice, and gave himself up to the problem of the track. It became easier when he branched right and the moon glided over the crags. He raced alongside the huge pile of shale and slate which marked the death at the turn of the century of a thriving and strenuous industry. Slivers of shale and slate had trickled down and hidden the path. They slid under his vibrams, and often he was groping with his hands over the shifting rubble. Then he reached the col, between Cnicht and the Moelwynians. He crouched forward and despite the half-light bounced and leapt down the running scree which led to the main track of the deserted village; slid down at a pace which if his nerves had not been taut with fear and anxiety would have plunged him head first on to the debris of a dying mountain.

Dr O'Neill had deliberately chosen and rebuilt the remote farm house towards which Simon, under a mesh of moonlight and stars, was running for a life. The doctor, a believer in the unspoken yet premeditated strangeness of being, met him with that courtesy which comes from a meditative solitude. Simon thought of Schwartz.

'I see, indeed I do see. We will take my jeep and I have the antibiotics, but first, since I imagine you have come faster here from Croesor, and at night, than anyone, you will drink this brandy.'

Simon murmured his thanks, tears of exhaustion welling from his eyes.

'If we are not here to be of use to each other, what are we here for?'

Then they were bumping down the track that led to Cwm Darn and the main track to Croesor. 'It's necessary to continue,' thought Simon. The stars were as bright as ever, the moon as swift under her racing cloud, the words of his wife as definitive. 'Don't let him come near me.'

The jeep swerved and rocketed over potholes covered with ice. Even before they entered the cottage the silence was audible. They tiptoed upstairs. Abbott was seated by Laura, holding her limp hand . . . he said nothing, but held up the thermometer.

'My God!' said O'Neill, for the thin line of quicksilver was over 105 degrees.

He held out the phial of antibiotics. Charles shook his head. The issue was not in their hands any more; it had gone beyond the powers of medication. Simon thought involuntarily of those hands by which, forever falling, we are upheld. They only could sustain her now. Quietly, he sat on the floor beside his dying wife, his hand close to her sweating body, but out of touch, knowing that in sleep lay her only chance of healing.

Laura opened her eyes and looked at Simon; it was both a valediction and 'then shall I know even as also I am known'—a gaze of total love and recognition.

He had slipped one hand behind his wife's head. She jerked forwards, tried to cough and then her eyes looked

through and far beyond him, beyond the cottage, beyond the
fell side and the sea. Before the fact of this death, Dr Abbott
had slumped forward in his chair and was bitterly weeping.

13

Requiem aeternam dona ei, Domine,
Et lux perpetua luceat ei.
Requiescat in pace.
Amen.

Abbott gripped his friend's hand as the gates opened
and the mortal body of the woman they both loved slid
towards the fire.

'I am the Resurrection and the Life. He who believes on
me though he is dead will live on; and whoever has faith,
to all eternity will not die.'

Simon clung to the words which affirmed the existence
of the wife he loved, loved as close as his own breath; she
had been the voice that always answered. Charred bones
were now being ground into fine dust by the rollers that
lay at the rear of the incinerator. He thought of Orpheus
coming back from the kingdom of the dead—followed by
his ghostly wife but glancing backwards for material reassurance. He knew that Laura still continued to exist within
and around him, and that only if he identified her being
with the used-up physical body he had known could she
appear to leave him. He heard Abbott speaking, 'No moment
of time is always. You will pass through this.' It is necessary
to continue.

Rhoda, asking no questions, was told no lies, but they
thought of Schwartz's 'old soul'. The child seemed aware of
every detail of what had happened but, knowing her own
limited capacity for endurance, she had passed it by in
order to live. She would live and she would help; she was
not strong enough to experience the finality of her bereave-
ment.

She sat in the front seat of the car between Charles and
Simon as they drove back to London. She seemed to realise
no chatter was relevant, but they felt she was trying to take
Laura's place by numerous little attentions. Rhoda straight-

ened their knives and forks in the roadside café, she poured tea, she took care that neither Simon nor Charles forgot a scarf or hat; she was being mother. 'They would say,' Abbott said to him, when they were alone together for a few moments, 'that she has introjected her mother, has made an identification to bypass loss. But it would be equally valid to say that her mother is present to lend a helping hand.'

'Indeed she is present,' said Simon through his tears.

As term wore on and they settled into a placid if narrow routine, it was his daughter that made Armstrong's life tolerable. He could not bear to enter those deeper areas of feeling that are the source of poetry. That would have meant reliving Laura's death and it was too close to be bearable. But he attended with new and almost pedantic thoroughness to the running of his department. Not writing, he also gave up much of his free time to the more difficult students. Scenting that he had endured similar difficulties to their own, they came to him not so much for advice—it has little value in such cases—but to air their problems to a sympathetic listener. There was Barbara Fry, the daughter of a distinguished journalist and a mother who made a great deal of money by imitating in bronze or plaster the fantastic shapes that the Atlantic had imposed on many boulders of the Cornish coast. She was a constant visitor, her main problem how to grow up and be her individual self under the overpowering shadow of her parents. There was Michael Halford, illegitimate, intelligent, sensitive. He had been adopted by two leaders of the Strange People. Sex was a forbidden word for this society, but since they desired children to convert to their nasty ethics and Mrs Halford secreted a vaginal spermicide, Michael was their fifth adoption. Two earlier efforts had ended up in Borstal, one in an Approved School, and one had disappeared; Michael was the only one who had stood up to the incessant exhortations and strappado of the righteous. Simon had managed to convince the youth that his step-parents were by no means typical of the general run of humanity. So

Michael played possum to their bullying, took the bait of reality and progressed to a degree and marriage.

Ian Vicars was a more devious problem. Though he was attentive at lectures and seminars, damp and ambiguous, Simon found his quiet odour of rectitude somewhat unwarranted and inaccurate.

'It's like this, Professor Armstrong,' he embarked on his complex embroidery. 'Now my poor wife was, in fact still may be, on heroin, 'horse' as they call it . . .'

'I am aware of that, Mr Vicars.'

'Oh, *are* you sir, I see. Now I'm not blaming her for that; she got into bad company and she's weak, very weak. The real trouble is that the future of our child is at stake; our two-year old boy. Believe me, sir, Vivienne is not the right person to look after him.'

'Then who is?'

Ian sniffed self-righteously. 'I am, sir; it is hard, but I can manage. But there's more trouble. I want to bring an action against my wife for her addiction, but if I do then she threatens to bring a counter-action stating that I am a homosexual.'

'Well, are you?'

'Really sir,' Vicars lisped, 'would I be confiding in you for help and guidance if I was one of those? I certainly am not. But she'll use any means, any, to get that child; she wants to make him an addict. Mind you, there was this boy . . .'

'What about him?'

'He was on his beam ends, you see, so I had him for a lodger on condition he helped me out with all the chores. Well, we did talk late and he was fond of me, poor child, but Vivienne had no right to say she found us . . . embracing. That's what the wicked woman said, sir, embracing.'

'Were you?'

'Professor, you are my personal tutor at my personal request,' Simon sadly recalled when this new planet had swum into his ken, 'you above all people cannot believe such wicked lies.'

'All right then, I don't, but Mr Vicars, if you don't want your case to be splashed over every newspaper in the country, then hang on until you can get a divorce for something respectable, like adultery.'

Another frequent visitor was Charles Yung Dal, a highly Christianised Chinese who had trouble with English Literature. Though fascinated by Donne, Shakespeare and Robert Browning, he found it hard not to believe that sex was some form of English sport like Cricket and Rugby Football. As president of the Christian Union he was organising a series of external lectures on 'Sex and the Christian' and needed a little help with his introduction.

There was also the 'long-haired brigade'. They were persona grata as far as his department was concerned, but many of them were training to be teachers and their flowing locks infuriated most headmasters in the schools where they did their teaching practice.

'I am sorry, Professor, but unless you can persuade him to get a haircut, I cannot have him in my school.'

He usually did manage to get some of the stuff off, but since the shearing was usually done by a girl friend, the final result was rarely pleasing. Anyway, long hair was, for the young, a symbol of liberty, some basic unity of male and female, a revolt too against paternalism. Considerable tact was needed to suggest that in a fallen world compromise was a necessity.

The line was unending; but at four-thirty, Professor Armstrong always collected Rhoda from school. They had high tea together and afterwards he corrected essays while she watched the telly. Then it was cocoa and bed. He had bought her a terrier pup for company and she enjoyed looking after it.

He only saw Abbott at lunch now and amid a 'rationalisation' of dons which made meaningful conversation impossible as one high IQ fenced furiously with another over some irrelevant detail of scholarship. He could not bear to seek out his friend in their old haunts where he had drunk and talked with Laura. But it was the penultimate day of term and Charles brisked into his room.

'So you are still alive!' he looked at Simon critically.

'Mildly so.'

'Look Simon, I want to talk to you. Make it this evening.'

'And Rhoda...?'

'I've done my field work. Rhoda is going to the Bursar's party, you know, it's his daughter's birthday.'

'Of course. She's been getting her finery ready for the past week.'

'Good, then we can have a drink; the party won't be over till nine p.m. Shall we make it The Rover, six-thirty?'

'Not The Rover, Laura and I used to meet you there regularly. Let's make it The Swan.'

'That tarted-up morgue. All right, but don't imagine Laura wants us to meet in that hive of stockbrokery. You will have to work through your mourning.'

'In my own time,' said Simon, as his wife stabbed at his heart, 'in my own time.'

At a quarter to six Simon decanted Rhoda at the Bursar's and was glad to see how gaily she mixed in with the other children. Charles was already in the chrome and plush 'Village' bar of The Swan, scowling darkly from behind his pint at the loudspeaker which, framed by plastic flowers, poured out a constant stream of canned music.

'Stay as sweet as you are, don't ever change, dear, I need you.'

'That last one was a beauty,' said Abbott, 'a perfect do-it-yourself recipe for a divorce within six months. Not to mention the one that came before, "I'd like to get you on a slow boat to China." You look pretty bleak though. I'll get you a pint, it will make the weather more clement, not that we have much chance in this sea of treacle.'

Simon drank deeply. 'The first for weeks.'

'Precisely,' Abbott replied, 'and that's what I want to talk to you about. This passivity—I'm speaking as a psychiatrist and I do know you better than most both clinically and from friendship, not that the two should be distinguished—you can't change your whole pattern of life and get away with it.'

'There is Rhoda, I have to look after the girl.'

'There are baby-sitters, and plenty of motherly souls who would be only too glad to look after Rhoda for a few quid a week. Much better for her, you don't want a "Daddy's girl" on your hands, dwindling into old-maidship. As far as I can see, Simon, you are trying to become an automaton. You don't write any more, you don't climb, you've stopped drinking. We used to meet at least once a week in The Rover, but for the last months we haven't exchanged more than a few platitudes in the Common Room. What's your programme? No, don't tell me. I bet it's good Dickensian Podsnappery. Getting up at seven-thirty, breakfast at eight, Rhoda to school, University at ten, more than double your usual number of tutorials, not to mention endless sessions with lame ducks who would be better off with a kick in the backside.'

'As you say; then Rhoda from school, high tea, cocoa, bed.'

'You sleep?'

'Very little, I'm catching up with the new theologians, Tillich, Bultmann, de Chardin. They're much more relevant than the Lit Crit boys. Of that I'm certain.'

'It's what's going to catch up with you,' said Abbott, looking through The Swan to some remote peak of brooding, 'yes, that's what I'm worried about. You can't go on living like this and not have an explosion. You postulate a full stop, but life isn't like that, you either go on or go backwards. The poet, all the vitality and chaos you lived through in your writing. That still exists. You're only ticking over on the surface but the energies are still inside you and some way or another if you don't use them they're going to find an outlet.'

'You mean, if I don't use them, then they will use me.' Simon pulled anxiously at his cigarette.

'Yes, and if you don't like them, they won't like you either. It's not pleasant to be ridden by the unconscious.'

'You're right, of course, but what's the remedy? If I try to write verse, then all I come back to is Laura in that room, coughing. It is too close, too painful.'

'Well then, get on with your *Cult of the Vampire*. That book was taking a great deal of yourself into it. How far have you to go?'

'About 25,000 words.'

'Then, I'm speaking professionally, get on with it and have it finished when I come back from the culture vultures in the States. That will be three weeks or so.'

'*The Cult of the Vampire*—Charles, I'm damn glad you winkled me out this evening, I'd almost forgotten that book existed.'

'It wants to exist, and if you don't get on with it then the energies which want you to write it, which in a sense are the book in potential, are going to give you a breakdown.'

'The book it will be. But it will be pretty dreadful writing all day, with no Laura for me to read it to in the evening.'

'Perhaps you'll be out of the wood when you've finished it. But don't get into a flap if I tell you something. Nobody knew better than I that Laura loved you, does love you, but I think she was frightened by your *Cult of the Vampire*.'

'She never told me that.' Simon looked up sharply.

'She told me. Laura had good cause to know about your vampire phobias; at least at the start of your marriage. She felt that in the book you were not only saying something of general meaning, but letting the vampires out into daylight, letting them loose on your pages. She thought, and in part I agree with her, that your writing would either free you from them, or that they would take over ...'

'Perhaps that's why I stopped writing. Isn't Rhoda in danger?'

'Not in the least. She has "the old soul", perhaps she dealt with the things in an earlier edition of herself. Don't you remember my little exhibition at Schwartz's? No, you're the one to worry about. You're strong enough, Simon, and you'll need to be, because in this book you'll be dealing with a psychosis. Few people do that; but get on with your book. It's the only way forward although it is dangerous.'

'Yes, I have no alternative and anyway, I feel delighted at the prospect of working again.'

'You couldn't go on repressing—Well, I must prepare for the States and you'd better be off to the Bursar's. By the way, you obviously won't be able to work in your Welsh cottage. Ask old Stoneham if you can have his cottage at Zennor for a few weeks. I know he's going to Venice and he wants to let it. It would be a damn good place to work in and what's more, there are lots of families about for the girl. He'll write you an introduction.'

14

Be near me when my light is low
   And the blood creeps, and the nerves prick
   And tingle; and the heart is sick
And all the wheels of Being slow.

Simon thought of Laura as he returned from a poetry reading. The extreme remoteness and closeness of the dead; few had expressed it with such power as Tennyson or captured so exactly the tension between doubt and faith. He would have enjoyed the reading if his wife had been there to talk about it with him. Montague Long had been there and relied for his punch lines and a few beery guffaws on a constant reiteration of four-letter words which had lost shock-voltage some fifteen years ago, with the possible exception of some far outpost of Poesie presided over by the leader of a Mothers' Union or a Rural Dean. Daniel O'Dee, a pundit of the radio, also peppered his works with oaths, but as an additional attraction there were constant references to blood and guts, and he had even got a girl to dance and mime his quieter pieces. If one did not listen to the verse the effect was charming.

Abbott had been away for two weeks now and although he had almost finished his vampire book, Simon felt lonely, but was too indifferent to stay and enjoy the literary chit-chat in the pub where he had read his poetry.

Be near me when I fade away
   To point the term of human strife
   And on the low dark verge of life
The twilight of eternal day.

He let himself into the house and was greeted by an exuberant baby-sitter.

'Oh good, Professor Armstrong, dead on nine-thirty as you promised.'

'Going to a party?'

'Goodness, what else?' she said, putting the standard fifteen shillings into a pocket of her scarlet trousers, 'I wouldn't career round like this otherwise.'

'Well, have a lovely time.' He smiled with pleasure at her young vitality.

'I certainly will, but do ask me again, Rhoda's been simply marvellous, we drew pictures together, talked and she certainly does talk, then bed and a story and now she's fast asleep.'

As she shut the front door, the telephone rang. Simon suspected and hoped it would be Stella. His hand trembled as he lifted the phone.

'It's me. I didn't ring you before because I felt you would want to be alone. How are you? It must have been terrible.'

'It still is.'

'I've felt it too. I wanted to ring you up . . .'

'I'm glad to hear you. How are you and how is Robert?' His hand was damp as he clenched the speaker.

'I've left him. Simon, I must come over and see you now.'

'But I thought you two were getting married?'

'It wouldn't have worked. We broke it off weeks ago. How is *The Cult of the Vampire?*'

'Almost finished; but it's hard work on my own.'

'Listen Simon, I do know this. If we lose our chance together, then I'll just drift, go hollow again, and you, believe me darling, you won't write another worthwhile book.'

'Hang on a moment.'

Simon went to the sideboard and poured himself a very strong gin indeed. He swallowed it down then lifted the receiver. 'Please come; I'm longing to see you.'

As he dropped off to sleep after a meeting so strong and irresistible that it seemed they shared a destiny, Simon thought of those dead lovers of myth who intermingled so completely in their acts of love that it was as if flame mingled with flame. 'Whatever happens,' he murmured, 'this has happened, it is part of our lives . . .'

'This will never cease to exist,' said Stella, 'never.'

She had woken before him in the morning and when he

went down to breakfast, wondering anxiously about Rhoda's reaction, the two of them were chatting happily over tea and scrambled eggs.

As Rhoda jumped up for him to kiss her he felt deeply relieved.

'This is Stella,' she said, 'and she says she's going to stay with us for good, may she?'

Again Simon thought of 'the old soul'.

'Well, I'll have to think about it.'

'You see Stella, that's his way of saying "yes".'

'Then if Stella's willing it's right for all of us; and I'm delighted.' His heart pounded with joy.

'One thing though, I forgot to tell you, I have to fly to Northborough this afternoon, to give a couple of kick-off lectures at a course they're starting at the University. The plane leaves Heathrow at one-thirty and I'll be back to-morrow afternoon.'

Rhoda grinned at Stella. 'And I was going to be looked after by Mrs Watson but now you're here and we don't need "Mrs Bristles." Ring her up, Dad, and say we don't need her now. She kisses me and she tickles and she smells of fish and I don't like her.'

After a morning which Stella and Rhoda spent shopping and Simon getting his lecture notes ready, they drove to the aerodrome.

'Bye Daddy, see you tomorrow,' said Rhoda, holding firmly on to Stella's hand.

'You see, darling,' Stella whispered, as she kissed him, 'It's going to work.'

The ancient Viscount gave out a shrill whistle as it rose skyward and an icy draught needled round the cabin.

'For Christ's sake, girl, I don't want to shoot with a wry neck, do something about this bloody typhoon.' A tweeded, bottle-nosed old warrior who had come aboard with two gun cases spoke for all the chilly passengers.

The air hostess swayed to the cabin and came back with the co-pilot. They conferred near Simon's seat and he overheard her saying, 'It'll be that wee leak again, Jock, can we fix it?' Jock was a man of resources. He went to a locker and brought out three large cartons of paper tissues.

H

With practised skill they proceeded to stuff these into a large tube. The whistle and draught subsided but there was a sensation when they came down on the airstrip. The port-side door was opened and an infinite number of tissues whirled round the Viscount in the blustering gale. From a distance they were indistinguishable from foam and two fire engines raced towards them.

Armstrong was met by the head of the English Department, Dr MacTavish. He was large, rugged and lantern-jawed. His obsession for work brought him to innumerable committees and he was now in charge of the entire administration of English Studies for the North. His passion was linguistics and the students under his care received plentiful and extremely unpalatable doses of what in more unenlightened days was called Grammar.

'Dr Armstrong, I presume?' he pumped Simon's hand and laughed uproariously, 'and welcome to the city.'

'My first visit too,' said Simon, thinking how much Stella would have enjoyed the expedition.

'Education and fish,' said MacTavish, as he drove swiftly to the College, 'there's no other industry, we've a Technical College, an Art College, a University and a College of Education. Would you be interested in linguistics, now?'

'Afraid it's not my line. I'm fairly specialised on Poetry and a few novelists.'

'A pity; it's a main feature of our courses up here. Poetry, Drama and the Novel are all very well in their places; but it's Structural English that gives them the stiffening.'

'Something to get their teeth into—like Sanskrit.'

'Sanskrit I had thought of, for a few chosen specialists, mind you. But you know what staffing problems are, it wouldn't have been economic.'

Simon glanced at him in wonder. Surely he must be joking, but there was no smile on his face; only a pucker of disappointment.

'Well, here we are, and we must meet the Principal, Dr Caithness; you'll know his work on the Gaelic. But he's not only a scholar, he's a Thespian, and will be wanting you to see our theatre.'

MacTavish was right; after a few words of welcome, the

burly Dr Caithness whisked them off to 'the finest theatre this side of Edinburgh, though I say it myself.' He was undoubtedly right, the Education Authority had poured money into the college.

'Look at the stage, revolving, mind you, and the panel of lights. It can only be worked by a specialist.'

Simon admired the innumerable buttons and dials and switches, more intricate than any aeroplane.

'What are your chaps putting on next term?'

'Would you believe it, they wanted some German thing called *Mother Courage,* by . . .'

'Berthold Brecht.'

'That's the name, but I dissuaded them. Our lads come from round here or as far as the isles and are a lot more tractable than your Southerners. No, it's to be *Lilac Time,* for a start, and then *The Mikado.*'

'Both drama and music, it will be an adventure.'

'Exactly; old favourites, but the right stuff. No tunes like the old tunes; but I can see Andy looking impatient there, he'll be wanting to take you back for one of Mrs MacTavish's famous teas.'

No. 2 Glencoe Avenue was done out in style. There were frilly china shepherdesses on the mantelpiece, embossed thistles on the wallpaper, photographs of their stalwart children and grandchildren and a large heart-shaped plaque, fitted out with sprigs of heather and bracken with sea-shell borders and a shiny coating of varnish.

Academic prowess, Simon thought, is by no means synonymous with aesthetics. But it was compatible with friendship; coming to Northborough he was treated as a member of the family to the last spoonful of Mrs MacTavish's excellent fish pie. But it was six-fifteen and his lecture was due to start at seven. He looked at his host. 'Well, only half an hour or so before my lecture, how about a drink?'

Mrs MacTavish beamed with pleasure. 'There you are, Andy, he's just like yourself, a devil for his tea. Wheesht a few seconds and I'll brew up for you.'

'Your tea was wonderful, but actually I—I was thinking

of something a bit stronger. You know it's been a longish day and a brace of pints would put me in voice for the lecture.'

The MacTavishes looked at each other in consternation.

'It's a wee bit difficult, you see we're teetotallers, the pair of us, and there's no' a public house between here and the University.'

'Oh yes, there is,' said Simon, 'I marked it on the way up, first left, second right, The Old Pretender.'

'But it's very rough you see. Wouldn't look right for us to go there. It's mainly for fisherfolk.'

'Nothing unrespectable about fishermen; at least the Gospel says so. Anyway, if you don't want a speechless lecturer, coats on and The Pretender.'

The MacTavishes were distinctly reassured by the polished horse-shoes, the shining mugs and, above the bar, the framed quotation from Robert Burns:

> O wad some po'er the Giftie gie us
> Tae see oursel's as ithers see us.

They appreciated the sentiment and admired the sprigs of heather that surrounded the coloured text.

The burr of conversation fell off slightly and tanned faces gazed admiringly as Simon sank three pints of beer in five minutes.

'The further north the better the bitter,' he grinned at a stout jerseyed sailor who had a creel of lobsters at his feet, their claws and feelers groping hopelessly through the wicker meshing.

'You're right there sir.' He glanced at Armstrong approvingly. 'A Londoner I take it, your first visit?'

'It is indeed and I'm starting to enjoy it. Armstrong's the name, Simon Armstrong.'

He noticed a large red-faced woman look up at him, take a little book from her pocket and turn the pages.

'Jock MacPherson, that's me. But pardon me sir, would that be Dr MacTavish of the University and his gude lady you have with you?'

'It is indeed, let me introduce you.'

The sailor bowed and shook their hands gently. 'This is

116

a great occasion sir. I've heard a lot about you from our Ian.'

'Ian MacPherson, is he your boy?' MacTavish's face creased with pleasure. 'A real asset to the department, a most promising linguist. Well Simon, we must be off.'

'Just one more.'

He noticed that the stout woman was nudging MacPherson. 'This one is on me, sir, and I'd be glad if you'd meet the Mrs. I think she knows about you from our other boy who's up at Oxford.'

He shook Mrs MacPherson's warm calloused hand, 'Are you the Mr Armstrong who writes the poems, you'll excuse my asking?'

'Yes indeed, but?'

She held out a small, well used copy of the current Golden Treasury. 'My son gave me this for Christmas and your poems, such a pleasure I've found them! If you could just sign by your name here.'

'I'm delighted.'

'Well, that's our town for you,' said MacTavish proudly, 'but now the College.'

Simon felt the usual angst as he sat facing some sixty earnest teachers while he was introduced. Their sharp pencils were poised and they were all avid for culture. He thought sadly of the warm bar of The Pretender. As usual, though, once he got to his feet the gear changed; he slipped out of the anxious persona of Professor Armstrong, became his theme and after an hour leant back for questions. There were plenty of them, many of them pointedly directed at MacTavish's insistence on linguistics. He passed these over to the good doctor who answered with such dogmatic fluency that the proceedings broke up by eight-thirty.

The vote of thanks and the applause was genuine but to Simon's disappointment—he would have enjoyed sampling more local pubs and conversation—the teachers melted away like snow and the MacTavishes whisked him round to the Caledonian Hotel.

'Coming in for some coffee?'

'Nine-thirty's late for us, Professor Armstrong, but a thousand thanks, dear man, you got the course off to a flying start. You did splendidly.'

'Well, thank you both for your hospitality and remember if ever you come to London, there's always a welcome.'

The bar of The Caledonian was large, plushy and deserted, although in the ballroom a dance was going on and there were skirls of pipes and the occasional war whoop. 'If only Stella were here;' as usual when drinking alone he took out a pencil and thought about for a poem. It must be a sort of postcard from the North and he would give it to Stella when they met tomorrow. Given an incentive the words came easily.

> Why in this stony city
> With the air as sharp as the knife
> Fishwives use to gut herring
> Is there so much cultural life?
> I mean there's a College for Teachers
> And a University,
> Not to mention a granite monster
> Of Domestic Economy.
> I have lectured for more than two hours
> On the meaning of poetry,
> But now that my stint is over
> There's no one to drink with me.
> The dons and the teachers have vapoured
> Wifewards away. To some ferns
> I chatter without conviction
> And am sorry for Robert Burns.

Stella will enjoy that bit of frivolous verse but, Christ, I wish she was here.

> O Lyric love! half angel and half bird—

But that was Browning's Invocation to his dead wife.

'When shall we three meet again,' he muttered, 'Yes, I do believe in "being" after death, "being" not "living". That's where all the trouble starts, projecting finite terms on to eternity. We will be born into death and Santayana's right. "Life is not a spectacle or an entertainment but an ordeal." '

When the hurly-burly's done
When the battle's lost and won . . .

'Then there will be the meeting. The meeting—there I go again, pushing finite terms onto the everlasting. Christ had an answer for this one, ambiguous as usual because he wanted to be accurate about human nature. What did he say to the Sadducees' trick question about the woman who'd been married seven times? "They which shall be accounted worthy to obtain that world, neither marry, nor are given in marriage; neither can they die any more: for they are equal unto the angels; and are the children of God, being the children of the resurrection." '

'Penny for them.'

Simon raised his eyes and saw first a large podgy hand, its flashy paste rings and silvered fingernails at odds with the soiled dish cloth with which it swabbed down his table. Next appeared a tightly stretched sheath of shiny black satin over a cushioned belly, a large besequinned bosom and finally the heavy, mauve powdered face of the bar mistress, the mouth painted like a grotesque kewpie-doll, blue mascara smeared over the pads of flesh from which two unwinking eyes regarded him with malice and curiosity.

'Daphne!'

'Not on your wee life; Flora MacGrotty's the name, and if you're not a resident or Bonnie Prince Charlie then it's closing time and out you go before I can say "Sassenach"!'

'I am a resident so perhaps we could have a drink before we turn in.' At least this was someone to talk to, however bizarre.

Flora MacGrotty pirouetted on stiletto heels, stepped back a pace, placed her hands on her hips and gazed down at him like a ringmaster. He noticed the bedraggled carnation stuck between her breasts, and felt like some aged creature of the circus who had lost any impulse to fight back. The woman was both formidable and, in the gold blue smokey lounge of the Highland Bar, strangely ghostly, like a sheath of ectoplasm. If he pinched that great fleshy thigh, would his fingers meet together as on soft paste?

'Turn in together, is it! The cheek of the—the indecency

of the bloody English; sex, it is, sex, sex!' She winked heavily, 'but I won't say no to a large whisky.'

As she oozed towards the bar, the orchestra struck up the signature tune of The Melting Pot and for a moment Simon saw Daphne and Stella sitting together in the club. He shook off the fantasy.

> 'I can't give you anything but love, baby
> That's the only thing I've plenty of, baby'

Flora crooned as she placed a tankard of beer beside him and gazed lovingly at her amber glass.

'You're brooding again, my wee man. What is it then? Trouble with the wife? Tell Mrs MacGrotty.'

She drew her chair close to his and placed one pudgy hand on his thigh.

'I'm the one for making you forget your troubles,' she winked again, and Simon drew back as her hand worked up towards his flies.

'Shy is it you are? But my wee lad, the number of gentlemen whose troubles I've smoothed away in this bar! What's more, the manager is out the night, so there's just the two of us.' She put one fat but surprisingly muscular arm over his shoulder, bent her dolly mouth close to his ear so that he could feel her warm whiskied breath and began to croon, 'You in all the world, just you, Yes, my bonny lad, me and you.' The silver-taloned hand pressed into his thigh and crept gently upwards. 'Why not?' For one moment something very crude and early flickered in his genitals. 'What does it matter, no one will know, it will be a temporary world's end.' Then he realised that what he really wished to do was urinate.

'Excuse me, Flora, but I must pay a visit.' He stood up and saw her eyes narrow, and flicker with annoyance.

'Go and have your wee-wee then, and Flora will set up the drinks; how about a shorty?'

'No, just the usual pint,' he felt the ringmaster's cord drop off him and thought of Stella's slim graceful body; what spell had he been under?

Flora MacGrotty was slowly revolving on the carpet when he returned from the lavatory, her jowls shaking gently as

120

she trilled and pirouetted, holding her glass before her as if it was her dancing man.

'She's not going to drink me!' he thought, and said 'Just this one and then I really must turn in.'

'What do you mean "I"? Now just sit down like a sensible wee man and we'll come to our understanding, you won't regret it, honey child, you won't forget Flora.'

Armstrong's voice chilled. 'What is there to understand? I've enjoyed our drink, but what else is there?'

'Don't you know?' Her wounded eyes winced back for a moment behind their pads of painted flesh, her mouth cringed sideways from its painted image. 'I shan't charge you if that's what you're worrying about.'

'That's not the real point, dear; I was alone tonight but I'm not unhappy; I have a woman friend and I'm very fond of her.'

'Then,' Flora MacGrotty's flower had sunk into what submarine depths, 'You are a prick teaser, a punk, a pansy boy who is frightened of a real woman.'

Her body jelled hard and vindictive from its teeetering ectoplasm, she hiccupped noisily. 'A pansy,' she spat into a bowl of artificial flowers and her spittle thick and viscous hung over the pot's green edge. 'What you want is to meet my man, Hamish...'

'I don't want anything. I've enjoyed our meeting, I've worked hard today at your college and I could do with some sleep.'

'You could do with having your arsehole tickled by my wee Hamish, he's a great one for the boys, though he likes them a lot younger than you, a great deal younger, that's why the police got him; bad cess to the panzoid bastards. Because Hamish is right...'

Flora MacGrotty was herself again and loomed down over him, her hands clenched and fisted on each padded hip, her eyes staring small and porcine between their bags of painted meat.

'Right, right, right I tell you! D'you think men and women understand each other? Shit-balls! I've had far better times making love to women than with any man. You prick, you nothing! I know what a real woman feels and I can make her feel like a woman and she can give me an orgasm quicker than you could if you worked away all night. All night, night, night, all night, nothing.'

'Oh God!' he thought, biting back his anxiety like sour bile. 'I'm back again with Daphne and Stella. How far had it gone before she got out of that huddle? The woman's a witch; she has brought it all home to me. Belly to belly, breast to breast, the sucking mouth, the furred tongue, the dill-doll or the skilled forefinger.' The faint light of The Highland Bar changed into the crimson doom light of The Melting Pot.

'I must speak to Flora MacGrotty, bed her, anything to prove it isn't true.'

No Flora was present; only a few sticky red-ended cigarette butts and a stink of cheap sweaty scent to mark the way of her passing.

But had Stella moaned with pleasure as she had done with him last night? Had she writhed and quivered to a finger or the fur and rubber contraption fixed to Daphne's thighs? Had she bent down her head and sucked at a moist vagina? Bats, bloody bats, vampires!

Professor Simon Armstrong walked upstairs to room fifty-three of the Caledonian Hotel at one-thirty a.m. on the third of July, his obsession hammering within him. 'She did, she didn't, she did, she did. Oh God, make it tomorrow so that I can get an answer. It's too late now, make it tomorrow. She did, she didn't, she did . . .'

When he turned out the light, these words and the image of Daphne and Stella, naked in a reversed embrace, seemed to hang from a great creepered tree and weave in and out of his intolerable slumber.

15

SIMON opened his eyes and remarked with pleasure the cold bright sunlight that filtered through the curtains of his room in the Caledonian Hotel. It was different from London, thin and clear as if one were thrust upwards into the sky. Then like a returning toothache, the experience of the previous night stabbed into consciousness. He dressed and shaved slowly, the pain of his obsession making every movement effortful as if he was in the grip of heavy influenza. His mouth was dry and he had to take repeated cups of coffee to swallow his breakfast bacon and egg.

'I know it's only a fantasy but that doesn't make it any less real.' Like an automaton, he smeared butter on a thin sliver of toast. 'It should be obvious she's not a Lesbian from the night we spent together, from the way she talks, from my feelings towards her. But what if she's bi-sexual, buttered on both sides, as it were?'

But that couldn't be true; he had known a girl like that once and near the climax of their intercourse she had murmured ironically, 'You are passionate, aren't you?' That one had soon gone completely over to her own sex. Well then, he told himself, that lets Stella out of it. There was no holding out or withdrawn irony in her response, he knew Stella had gone towards him with the entirety of herself. It was impossible to deny the completeness of the journey they had made in their shared body.

Like toothache his obsession pierced the truths of experience. He must speak to her. Knowing well that the telephone is an unusually poor means of communication, he went to a phonebox, dialled his home number and waited for Stella's voice, his hand trembling on the receiver. What if she were out; had left Rhoda with some baby-sitter and spent a night at The Melting Pot?

'Stella Johnson here,' her voice came serenely to him over the contracted distance.

'It's Simon, love, how are you both?'

'It's lovely to hear you. I've scarcely been alive these hours and last night without you was awful.'

'Something rather horrible happened in the hotel last night...'

'You're not ill? Did the lecture misfire?'

'Nothing like that, no, it was in the hotel bar after the lecture, I met a woman exactly like Daphne.'

'How unpleasant, love! I trust you took the briskest avoiding action.'

'It's not her, it's what she's touched off in my mind that's horrible.'

'Whatever is it?'

'Don't you know?' His voice rasped over the phone.

'How can I, when you haven't told me? Did she crown you with a bottle or was she just bitchy?'

'I said it wasn't her, it's what she touched off in my mind. Tell me and don't lie; how far did you go with that Daphne?'

'I've told you before and you've no least need to worry. I went nowhere at all, except that foul night in The Melting Pot when you helped me.'

'Daphne acted as if she owned you...'

'Then that was her fantasy, it was not my responsibility.'

'Did you ever sleep together, do things together?'

'God, Simon, how could I have done? You should know me, especially after our night together. You must know...'

'I keep getting horrible pictures.'

'Then they're from yourself. They have nothing to do with me, I swear it.'

'Thank God!'

'Don't sound so melodramatic all those miles away in Northborough. I'll meet you three o'clock, Heathrow, and I'm longing to see you. As for your bad dream, we must talk it out when Rhoda has gone to bed. Loving is understanding, and I know we can deal with your nightmare, the two of us. Till then, sweetheart, have a look at the sea while you're filling in time for your plane. There's nothing more therapeutic than a harbour.'

'She's right,' thought Simon, as he mooched round the quays in the few hours before his plane's departure.

At first he only realised how depression, the fear of a loss of love, or the loss of the identity of the beloved, could bleed the world white and leave it devoid of meaning. But gradually, the sharp salt of the North Sea replenished his blood, the wash of shingle and the voracious scream of gulls silenced his obsession. He saw the endless elaboration of mussels and below them, sucked fast to the wave-worn stones of a jetty, long yellow brown streamers of kelp weaving up and down on the retreating water. He also was balanced between air and water, doubt and certainty, grief and joy, fantasy and reality, even—though this did not enter the bright circle of recognition—sanity and madness. The paired emotions cancelled each other out and left his mind free to an exceptional clarity of awareness. He saw the cruel, quicksilver flash of the fisherwomen's knives as over long wooden troughs they gutted cod, hake, herring and offered the scarlet entrails to the gulls which exploded over the harboured water. He walked past the high-prowed trawlers where sailors mended perpetual nets or scraped rust and salt from sea-worn metal. There were stinking tubs of herring-roe and from the final stones of the wall he could see a black reef appear and disappear in the tide wash ... Too expensive to dynamite, it took its yearly toll of fishing boats and at low tide fostered a priestly population of shag and cormorant.

His obsession dwindled in the seascape.

> Not poppy nor mandragora,
> Nor all the drowsy syrups of the world
> Shall ever medicine thee to that sweet sleep
> Which thou owest yesterday ...

But you can't have modern Othellos, he thought, tasting the salt on his lips—not in this age of psychiatry. Tragedy must be the most strenuous act possible, given the data about some particular experience at a particular time. Nowadays it would be an arduous course of psychoanalysis, not paranoid jealousy, wife murder and suicide. The latter would have the smell of the medical case book on it and that goes for you, Simon Armstrong with your Flora

MacGrotty and Daphne fantasies. 'Not poppy nor mand-
ragora' . . . what if they put Shakespeare into modern English
like the ghastly modern versions of the Bible!

> Not sodium-amytol, not valium
> Nor all the most effective tranquillisers in
> circulation
> Will get rid of your obsession.

A crested shag dived from its clerical brethren and after
a few seconds surfaced on a further wave. Could he learn
from these creatures to merge into the outgoing impulse
of his own life, to know that unity which having been lost
by consciousness could only be regained by a further reach
of awareness?

It was time now. He caught a chilly bus to the airport
and was soon fastening his safety belt as the plane roared
for its take-off. The moment of truth occurred and the town
slid sideways behind him as the Viscount swept through
obliterating veils of mist into clear evening sunlight. Clouds
lay below him in a level tumble of white and pink ranges.
Was he also, as he swung out to London from the Northern
city, leaving his ghosts? No; as constant as the texture of
skin or the in- and outgoing of breath, until finally harrowed,
they must remain with him.

Slipping through brief reaches of cloud he knew that
Daphne, Flora MacGrotty, his dreams of vampires and the
werewolf were still his constant companions in a self-
begotten twilight.

Now Scotland and its crinkled metallic sea was far behind
him. The plane swung over Birmingham and on to London,
eating up time and space with its well-proven engines. One
had achieved an ampler material vision and further scienti-
fic information than ever before, seen space as thought and
thought as space; but there remained—more unexplored
than the Nile or Congo to the Victorians—the intricate
and ambivalent energies of the mind and heart.

Now the plane slid towards the intricate glitter of
London. He fastened his safety belt to the cooing demand
of the air hostess and thought of Dylan Thomas swigging
whisky high over Newfoundland. 'It was only my iron will

that kept that bird in the skies.' It was one's entire sub-
mission to an impersonal process that made landing exciting.
The plane dipped and merged with the grass of Heathrow.

For a time free of his ghosts, Simon walked towards
Reception and was soon greeting Stella and Rhoda with
unmitigated delight. As he looked into their clear warm
faces he was back again with reality.

He swung the car through the tunnel and onto the
motorway.

'Steady on, darling! You're doing over eighty and this is
a restricted area.'

'Good God,' he said, slackening his foot on the accelera-
tor, 'I was brooding about the lecture and I drive like an
idiot when I think about anything but driving.' He slowed
down to the appropriate 40 mph limit.

'But the lecture went well?'

'Perfect, except that you weren't there with me. You'd
have liked Andrew MacTavish...' He stopped speaking
and jerked back the image of Flora MacGrotty.

'What's the matter, Daddy?' asked Rhoda, 'why don't you
tell us about that woman?'

Simon looked at her. 'What do you mean? I only mentioned Andrew MacTavish.'

'But you were going to say someone else, I know that she
was beastly, that's why you are looking so cross.'

'Right, pet,' he said, thinking again of Dr Schwartz. 'I
did meet a Mrs MacGrotty, she was the bar woman, she was
fat and rude and I didn't like her.'

'Did you want to kill her?'

'He probably did,' Stella answered, 'it's surprising the
number of people even the nicest of us want to kill from
time to time. But we don't kill each other, thank goodness,
we're just rude and clear off.'

Back at the house they had laid out a splendid supper.

'This is better,' he helped himself to another trout, 'than
Mrs MacTavish's fish pies.'

'What were they like?' Rhoda asked.

'Mashed potato, lots of it, and steaming minced cod,
garnished with parsley and artichokes—very sustaining but
... there's the telephone—will you answer it?'

'I'll go,' Rhoda grinned as she skipped off and they heard her best telephone voice, 'Gladstone 0111, yes, Mr Armstrong is at home, who shall I say please?'

For a few seconds before Rhoda returned, Simon was also absent. The Melting Pot whirled about him and in shadowy corners he saw bodies twining together and heard the high-pitched twittering of women's laughter.

'It's the Vice-Chancellor's wife, and she wants you and Stella to come to supper tomorrow night . . . Daddy, what have you done to your fork?'

Simon surfaced from his apparitions and saw that the fork he was holding with both hands was bent into a semi-circle.

'I don't know, I was daydreaming; who was it?'

'It's Lady Nevis, and she wants you to come to supper tomorrow night.'

He turned to Stella. 'Please make excuses, darling, tell her I'm working on my new book and have almost finished. That's true anyway and she's a devil for a bit of culture.'

He noticed that Rhoda was still staring at the bent fork and tried to reassure her. 'I must be dead tired, or I wouldn't have played such a silly trick.'

'Why have you got such an angry face?'

'I haven't, really I haven't, I'm not angry,' he lied, 'just tired. Tell me what you read last night.'

'The Fisherwoman's Daughter, and the Talking Horse and the one about a man who turned into a wolf, very scary.'

'Well, it's Dad's turn tonight,' said Stella, coming back from the phone; 'I'm for The Protectors . . .'

'I want to watch the telly as well please; just tonight, I want to watch the telly.'

'But you'd got it all planned out, Dad was going to finish the last story.'

Rhoda looked at the bent fork and began to whimper, 'Please, please, let me watch the telly.'

'Of course, you've no school tomorrow and can stay up a bit late to celebrate.'

After The Protectors was finished and Rhoda tucked up safely in bed, Simon poured Stella a vermouth and for himself half a tumbler of neat gin. As he drank he felt the old horrors and fury seep back into his mind, his eyes redden as the gin bit down into his stomach. When he turned towards Stella, his face was no longer that of the man she knew. It was a blank mask and hatred stared from the eyeholes in its grey surface.

'Well . . . what have you got to say for yourself?' Even his voice was alien, a croak, which some still undrowned element of himself heard as from a great distance.

'What do you mean, why are you looking at me like that, what's come over you?'

'A desire to know the truth, the truth, the bloody truth, do you hear?'

'Of course, but honestly I don't know what you are talking about, for God's sake keep hold of yourself!'

'I want to know,' he rasped very precisely, his lips hardly moving, the voice of an automaton, 'I want to know what really happened between you and that bitch Daphne.'

'Nothing.'

'Don't lie to me, I want to know what happened?'

'Nothing, except what you saw in The Melting Pot, nothing except that!'

The palm of his right hand whipped out at Stella's mouth, whipped out and sent her reeling against the wall, her lower lip bleeding. He came on towards her, hunched and muttering, 'Lying bitch, I've been told by someone who knows you lived with her like man and wife, as lovers.'

He spat at Stella who, white-faced and trembling, got behind the table. Simon continued to shuffle forwards.

'You sucked each other off, she had a dill-doll, a dirty great rubber cock, rubber with fur round it, fur stained with shit. You prefer women to men.' He raised his hand to strike again. 'Cheat!'

'Don't touch me,' Stella cried, 'it's not true, it's not, Simon, don't touch me.'

'You allowed her to touch you, kiss you, kiss your cunt, put her tongue up your lug-hole. I'll teach you, Lesbian sow.'

At last Stella knew the terror of his obsession. Simon came on, his mouth open and dribbling, his eyes devoid of any expression but a single destructive intention ... She, who had been brought up a Catholic, also lapsed into automatism. She picked up a silver candlestick, and moving it before her in the sign of the cross uttered words she had rarely heard.

'In nomine Patris, et Filii, et Spiritu Sancti extinguitar in te omnis virtus diaboli, per omnium sanctorum Angelorum, Patriarcharum, Prophetarum atque omnium, simul Sanctorum. Amen.'

Simon stopped and blinked his eyes like someone waking from sleep or ether, his face wrinkled then twitched back into its human life again. 'Where am I,' he said, 'why is your lip bleeding, what has happened?'

Stella felt herself sweating and cold as she swallowed her glass of vermouth.

'It's all right,' she stammered, 'I haven't come to any real harm.'

'But your lip is bleeding, who has hurt you?'

She felt ice congeal in her blood, knowing that Simon was quite unconscious of what had happened, had blacked out.

'You don't know what has happened, you don't realise why I'm frightened, why my lip's bleeding?'

Simon's face was drained of blood and meaning. 'It's one of those attacks I used to have years ago, I remember ... saying goodnight to Rhoda and then nothing else till now.' He looked at his watch. 'Almost an hour has slipped me; please tell me what I did.'

'You drank some gin, then your face went quite empty, you cursed me horribly, you slashed out at my lip, you were coming on then ...'

'Then?'

'I made the sign of the cross with this candle I'm holding and said words from the liturgy of Exorcism. That did stop you, your whole face changed, you seemed to wake out of nightmare and be yourself again.'

'It's been one of those attacks. It isn't enough to say I'm sorry. I am terrified.'

'So am I, but I do believe that together we can deal with these attacks. We must understand. It's possession, something takes over,' Stella panted out, 'You were not you; a part of yourself, some savagery which you are too frightened of to bear, had taken over. Love, I think that this creature —I say creature, because you didn't even look like yourself —wants to kill me.'

Simon felt dizzy and without hope as if he had been a murderer in some previous life and the old pattern was trying to repeat itself.

'Abbott's right,' said Stella, 'as far as he goes. Your mother hated masculinity, was frightened of it and therefore wanted to geld you into a kind of girl-boy. As he says, part of your Lesbian phobia is the feeling you got from your mother, that a woman is more attractive to a woman than a man. It's a complex of perverse feeling. But what I saw a few moments ago and what I want to understand is the energy, the ferocious energy which teamed up with your repression and gave it power to dominate your whole mind and ordinary pattern of feeling. But I'm not sure that psychiatry can understand the power which joins up and wants to kill, because the horror which possessed you does want to kill my love, kill me because you love me. That power hates me so deeply because you love me, more intensely than anyone before.'

'There's only one way out,' Simon murmured, looking at his hands as if they might be ingrained with blood, 'understanding and being able to use this energy for a life purpose. You're right about mother; as 'man and woman' attraction goes, the male came a great deal second. What is more she kept me in girl's clothes, or something damn like them, until I was over five . . .'

'I know all that. But at least get one thing into your head, Daphne has no attraction for me at all, but you have; infinitely. Do realise that, except for a comparatively small number of "bent" females, among whom I most certainly cannot be included, your mother was entirely wrong about the sexes.'

Simon listened and with new hope to her strong, emphatic voice.

'I think that thanks to you, we may manage to reach the centre of the maze—and deal with this creature.'

Later that night if they had not been drawn so deeply into their single embrace, they might have heard from an infinite distance that was as close as their own heartbeats a thin twittering. They might have realised that the vagrant, parasitic energies which had settled into their life could not be exorcised by mere understanding and were almost as strong as their love.

They both woke in the small hours from a shared nightmare and Simon was shouting. When they switched on the light they saw Rhoda standing in the bedroom door looking very frightened.

'I heard you shouting, you *were* shouting and I'm frightened.'

'Come, darling,' Stella hugged the little girl, 'everyone has dreams and we have both had a nasty one; but it was only a dream.'

'Why only a dream?' Rhoda queried as after hot chocolate and consolation she was tucked up in bed again. 'Why is a dream only?'

'That last I cannot answer,' said Simon, when they were alone again. 'But this is terrifying. I think that in these next weeks we can only be safe if we realise there is no safety. We must be constantly watchful. Partly because of you, and because I do indeed love you, partly because I have finished my vampire book, it looks as if I have at last unloosed the demons. The question is, can I deal with the unloosed creatures or will they deal with me and, incidentally, with you, my own darling?'

As he dropped to sleep, he turned over in his mind an old negro spiritual which had been popular when he was at college.

I went to the mountains but mountains wouldn't hide me;
   No hiding place, anywhere there.
No hiding, no hiding, no hiding anywhere there.

16

THE NOVELIST Miles Milford was an active pederast. To his
somewhat overpowering personality could have been laid
the deaths of two youths, if one failed to realise that they
were veered to suicide as a compass needle to the North,
and Miles no more the cause than a gaspoker or bottle of
barbiturates.

He was tall, had a vestigial hare-lip and was impossibly
and often inaccurately erudite. He was indifferent to his
personal appearance and would arrive at literary functions
decorated with a blend of blood, egg and snuff. Besides this,
he was one of the most distinguished novelists of his time
and when not geared into his perversion, showed a concern
for others and indifference to his personal comfort which
accorded with some precepts of the Gospels. Like that of
Christ, his Christianity did not preclude a witty and vitriolic
tongue.

On the day of one of Miles' famous parties, to which
they were invited, a friend from the Italian Institute rang
Simon and Stella and asked if they would look after an
Italian acquaintance for the day.

'It's Richard Roland, darling, and he wants to know if
you'll look after Carlo Rossi. He's quite nice—I knew him
at Padua. He has the chair of Italian there.'

'Of glottology to be precise, whatever that means. I met
him three years ago when he was visiting the University.
We could take him to Milford's, they should get on, they're
both impossibly erudite. Anyway, now we're married we
can all lunch at High Table. It will be reassuring to have
that high-powered extrovert booming around the campus.'

Stella picked up the telephone. 'Yes, Richard, but we're
going to a party at Milford's tonight and you do realise
that despite his family portraits and Sheraton furniture
there'll be cigarette ash in the sandwiches, sardine tins on
the sofa, not to mention a rind of antiquity on the glasses.'

'May I assure you, my dear Stella,' said Roland, 'Professor Rossi will care for none of those things. He would like to meet some English writers and he would like to visit the College. He is also fond of music and I believe there is a concert in the Nelson Room at twelve o'clock. It's only eleven now so if I shove him into a taxi he can easily make it.'

'Well briefed at the Institute, aren't we! All right, then we'll meet him eleven-forty-five at the main entrance.'

Professor Carlo Rossi, the international authority on glottology, never forgot a face, and, whatever city he visited on his scholastic journeys, was always punctual. Portly, immensely confident and with a small beret perched on his massive balding head, he greeted them like an amiable polar bear.

'Simon and the Signorina née Johnson, now Signora, no Meesis Armstrong, my one short time collage—no *colleague,* in Padua, ciao, and how do you now?'

'Ciao, Carlo—it's "how do you do"—' Simon remembered affectionately Rossi's passion for languages, and that it was more a question of structure than colloquial speech.

'How do you do!' Carlo again shook their hands. 'And now', he nodded with delight at the phrase, 'do as the Romans do when in Rome; we have just time for a Guinness at the Pubblica. That is the English custom like tea?'

'It certainly is not.' Stella noticed that the Professor looked disappointed; 'you shall have several Guinnesses after five-thirty; now you're going to hear a concert of Elizabethan madrigals and there'll be sherry and lunch afterwards.'

'Madrigal,' Carlo rumbled like an exuberant dictionary as they walked to the Nelson room, 'Italiano-madrigale, from La madre, sempre la madre? but, aspettiamo! mandria, a shed for the cattle, a song of herd-sheeps.'

'Shepherds,' said Simon, piloting Rossi to a seat, 'but they're just going to begin, so sit down and shut up.'

Rossi bent forward, 'Shut up, what is the "shut up"?'

'Taci and taci subito or we'll be unpopular.'

The group was soon in full song but though fond of

music the Professor desired both aesthetic experience and information.

'Fine knacks for ladies,' sang the counter-tenor.

It was too much for Carlo.

'Knacks, knacks, what is "knacks" please?'

'Piano' whispered Stella, 'piano, più tardi.'

'Hush,' came from students behind them.

'Hush,' muttered Carlo, 'hush, the onomatopoeia, the great universal language of sound words.'

Simon delivered a brisk kick at the Professor's well padded shin. He took the hint and was silent for the rest of the concert.

The Master of the College was devoted to Italian poetry and was hoping to chat with Carlo about some of his favourites. The response of his distinguished visitor was not encouraging.

'Si, Rettore, Carducci, un grande poeta italiano, dell' ottocento,' Carlo steered the conversation back to more serious topics. He pointed at the table dishes, 'Here we have the "beans".'

'Exactly, Professor.'

'And here is the salad?'

The Master nodded dolefully.

'But I drink the bare ... the beer,' Professor Rossi held up his glass to the astonishment of High Table and, beaming with satisfaction, enlarged on the etymology of its contents, 'I drink the beer, you lie on the bier, but on the Lido at Venice I lie baare ...'

'I sincerely hope you don't,' said Stella, but Carlo was in full spate and oblivious to flippancy.

'Bare, bear, I bear your burden, and there,' he waved generously to the further end of the table. There we have the "small beer".'

'Professor Rossi,' said an unwary lecturer, 'I believe you are an authority on the Venetian language.'

'Si,' he bowed modestly, but there was a glitter in his eye; England was one of the few countries in the world who paid small interest to his study.

'Would you say that it contains many loan words from the Arabic?'

135

'Porca miseria!' Carlo exploded, 'have I not myself written *Arabian Loan Words in the Venetian Dialect?* Arabian, Turkish; Alkool, Alchemist, Algebra, all are the loan words. Like your English it is the hoacher-poacher!'

'Hotch-potch,' said Simon, 'and piano, you're not addressing a school of violent fellow-glottologists in Bucarest.'

'Hotch-potch, hotch-potch,' he relished the word, then filed it in under the correct letter of his memory, 'but si, Simon, I must cultivate the English "flam".'

'Phlegm's the word,' said Stella, 'one of the four humours, phlegmatic, of the earth.' They had retired to the Senior Common Room now and were finishing their coffee.

'Of the earthy, the person who is not to be moved, who is of a heavy natura.'

'Exactly, but drink up, we must be going.'

Professor Rossi said goodbye to the Master and Dean, with that courtesy and friendliness which had gained him affection in most of the capitals of Europe. 'Thank you, Rettore, grazie mille, for your so lavish hospitality. You have me made most happy, never shall I forget your kindness or your college.'

'Well Carlo, see you at six for a Guinness before the party starts, the Hand and Flower pub at Notting Hill, I should take a taxi.'

'No, Simon, an autobus I will try, to practise my English.'

They watched his indomitable figure shouldering off to the British Museum.

'I bet he does,' said Stella, 'and I bet he asks change for a five-pound note and gets away with it.'

When they arrived, Carlo was already leaning monumentally on the bar of The Hand and Flower, practising his English with no scrap of inhibition, on two of the locals. That these suspicious and for the most part anti-foreigner inhabitants of Notting Hill Gate were answering his questions with good-humoured interest was another tribute to the Professor's geniality.

'Ciao Stella, ciao Simon, what will it be?' he mouthed the new phrase with relish.

'Nice to see you, Carlo; a Guinness for me please, and a gin and tonic for Stella.'

'Bene, two of the Guinness for myself and my friend and a gin with the tonic for the lady.'

After one more round they walked off through the drab streets to Miles Milford's flat. For his own particular reasons the novelist was devoted to this shabby and somewhat savage district. It was darker than Soho and less police-haunted, but the same anonymous little groups hovered at street corners, or in front of unpainted decaying doorways. Hand in hand, two youths of unpredictable sex slouched past them, a small shine of white face glinting from each mass of uncombed hair; there was a roar of Irish voices from a small cider house and some children crouched round a smoky bonfire on a patch of ground still unclaimed from the blitz on London.

'Ah,' sniffed Carlo, 'the English cooking,' as they fumbled up badly-lit stairs to Milford's flat through a reek of grease and stale cabbage.

'You didn't tell me the half of it,' said Stella, as they surveyed the company, 'Meet the Munsters. It's like a carnival I went to in Trinidad, only this time there are no masks, these are real faces.'

'Well, look at it closely, because you won't see its like again, this is the last round-up of an era.'

Like a bloated Adjutant Stork, Miles Milford was the centre piece. His vestigial hare-lip was blurred by the party smoke haze but his harsh voice sliced through the noise of the crowd. Jimmy Lawrence, his current boy friend, hovered beside him. A failure of the public school system, without O or A level qualifications, or any drive towards conventional occupation, he supplemented his small remittance from home by lodging with Miles. No doubt he also hoped that the dominating writer might steer him into some pleasant job, something with the BBC, for instance, or even help him to pass some examination. It was unlikely; where his brand of sex was concerned, Miles was intensely possessive and had no least desire to help his protégé to those wings which might enable him to fly off and away.

'Take this,' he drawled to the stooping crew-cut youth, 'and get two bottles of Cinzano Bianco. Oh, and remember,' he stabbed the words home, 'I've given you a five-pound note, not three singles; I expect the right change and don't want to be diddled like last time.'

Simon and Stella noticed how the drained, high-boned face of Jimmy Lawrence flushed for a moment of humiliation and despair as he scuttled off on his master's errand.

'God help that one!' said Simon, looking with compassion at Miles' catamite.

'Somebody ought to,' said Stella, 'but the way he trembles, his stoop, those pathetic jackboots! I see no sign of hope.'

'Simon and Stella, lovely of you to come,' Miles seized two large smeared tumblers of red wine and slopping the liquid carelessly upon his guests, bored towards them.

'Here you are! everyone's come tonight . . .'

'Miles, this is Professor . . .'

The novelist would never halt when following his own line of conversation. 'As I was saying, everyone's here, even the last of the old narcotic squad. Look, there's Mrs Payne, glittering, she started to run down a few minutes ago and has just been to the lav for another shot in the arm.'

They watched the slim figure of Mrs Payne glide through the guests to a large woman in brogues and Irish tweed who was now her constant companion. The beautiful bones of her face seemed to be covered only by a thin layer of skin, her eyes were daubed under by green paint, her mouth a sharp streak of scarlet in the chalky whiteness.

'Still, not at all bad for sixty, and after a couple of decades of coke and heroin. Miles, I want to introduce you to Professor Carlo Rossi of the University of Padua.'

'Rossi, Rossi,' Milford flicked through the pages labelled R in his encyclopaedic mind, 'Rossi, Professor Rossi and *Arabian Loan Words in the Venetian Language*. Simon, have you no scholastic standards?' He turned to Rossi, 'If I'd known you were coming, I'd have asked Dr Jerk along, really he's the only serious person we've got in your field.'

Carlo bowed with pleasure. 'It is to be delighted and I too am most familiar with your magnificent translation of the poet, Carducci.'

'Let me get you a drink, and yes, there is someone I'd like you to meet, Professor Chad Harmon from Bison.'

Carlo was completely indifferent to the pantomime figures

that swirled around him. 'Harmon, Bison? I have him,' he beamed with happiness at a new phrase, not realising its suggestions might be offensive, 'he is the "small beer" but yes, I will wish to speak to him, there are some American corruptions in which I have interest.'

'You go steady with him, no bulldozing,' said Stella.

'Bulldozing?'

There was no time to satisfy Carlo for Miles was back, in one hand a glass of vermouth—Jimmy had done his stuff—in another a small timid, gold-spectacled trans-Atlantic don.

'Harmon, Professor Carlo Rossi of Padua.'

'Come, we will talk,' Carlo bore off his victim and very soon they could hear a steady stream of American and Italian phrases purring from the depths of a sofa.

'Selfish sod,' said Stella, 'I trust he sits on a sardine tin, still I'm extremely fond of Rossi. He could walk happily through the fires of Hell if there was a fellow glottologist or two to talk with.'

They looked at the other guests. 'This,' Simon murmured, 'is the end of a certain element of the Thirties, but look at Stephen Osgoth—him, to quote Carlo, I cannot stomach.'

Like a minor but very nasty demon, Stephen was standing in a quiet corner of the room alone, but his black beady eyes were fixed on a stout white-haired millionaire. The owner of a newspaper concern and a fish canning firm, Rath shared the erotic tastes of Miles Milford. It was all they had in common, but as binding as the shared membership of some exclusive club. At the moment the tycoon was gazing soulfully at a very pretty youth from one of the freer public schools whose white lacy shirt hung over a pair of striped silk trousers. As Stephen walked slowly towards them, Simon beckoned Stella to follow and they watched the tableau unnoticed.

Stephen touched Rath on the elbow, 'Excuse me, Mr Rath ... sir.'

The millionaire was not used to an unpremeditated appointment, 'What the hell d'you want? Can't you see I'm busy?'

'Yes,' said Stephen, the barb of a CID man in his quiet voice, 'I can see that you are busy; it's quite obvious to everyone, very busy indeed, but I'm afraid I must interrupt you.'

Rath took a pudgy hand from the knee of his young friend and looked at Stephen with the timidity of a plump rabbit. 'Well, young man,' he blustered, 'What the hell are you after?'

'I'm not after anything, that is not at this precise moment, but I do have something to say to you.'

'Well, then get on with it. I haven't got all evening.'

'It won't take all evening, not this evening anyway, but if you could come aside with me, and leave your ... "little friend", it might be more ... tactful.'

Simon and Stella also came nearer, but the stoat was too busy playing with its rabbit to notice them.

'I'm really on your side, sir, a well-wisher. I want to help you.'

'Why the devil should I need your help, you—you—'

'I shouldn't swear, Mr Rath, it won't help you one little bit. What I'm trying to say is, you just can't behave in the way you are behaving and get away with it. I do happen to represent a certain authority, and, believe me, that authority has had you under observation for a very considerable time.'

Almost one could hear the hissing sound as the tycoon subsided.

'But what have I done, what are they after, why are they concerned with me?'

'I think, sir, that you can best answer those questions yourself; I have merely come from the people I represent, as a warning, as a well-wisher.'

'Well-wisher, my foot,' Simon's intervention was not entirely altruistic; Stephen had for several years reviewed his work splenetically in a number of journals. 'No, sir, you are neither dealing with a well-wisher nor the representative of any authority except a very unpleasant little creature called Stephen Osgoth.'

'Damn you, Armstrong, this isn't your bloody business,' Stephen grasped a flask of Chianti, then remembered a previous encounter with Simon which had gone by no means well, and replaced his weapon.

'Let me introduce you, Mr Rath, this is Osgoth, reviewer,

thief and, in all probability, a homosexual who since he cannot admit his, pardon the word—perversion—spends his time annoying people; goodbye, Stephen.'

'Bravo, Sir Galahad,' said Stella, drinking her wine, 'mind you, though he's now distinctly dewy-eyed, Rath is an unusual maiden in distress.'

'Listen to the bastard!' There was a small explosion as Stephen left the party; he had smashed down the full Chianti flask on Milford's hall table.

They walked back to refill their glasses. A weather-beaten sixty-year-old, her lips painted into a large smudgy cupid's bow, was balanced delicately on the knee of a gross drunken Silenus who announced from minute to minute, 'Get up, you skinny bitch, and fetch me another glass of whisky.'

Miles spoke over Stella's shoulder, 'Really, I can't understand it. Heterosexuality is a complete mystery to me. Look at that, for instance! He's fat, he's extremely ugly, he's very nearly always drunk, he has, I believe, several very nasty diseases, yet he's strong enough despite it all and beats that extraordinary woman every other evening, and she seems to relish him . . .'

'Human nature,' murmured Stella.

'It's all very well for you, Stella Armstrong, but you don't have to live under his flat. I do, and when the party's over the whole house will be rocking. She's got a scream like a steam whistle too; we had the police in the other night. "Does the place no kind of good" as Eliot put it. Oh, there's Father Cowling, come and meet him.'

As Father Cowling was the chaplain of his college, Simon and Stella needed no introduction, although Miles performed it with ceremony.

'I've just come from a most delightful christening,' beamed the cleric. 'How nice it is to be among men of the arts! In your own curious way, though revolutionaries, you still keep to the old traditions, keep the faith, if I may say so. It was John Phillips—you know, the art critic—his little son, yes indeed, a most touching ceremony, the mother so young, the father mature, both full of hope, God bless them.' Father Cowling sniffed into his scented handkerchief.

'If,' said Miles, 'as I suspect, you're talking about the

watering of Phillip's recent brat, then I was there too, though you didn't choose to notice me; what with Dean Rockwood, not to mention Lord and Lady Havenheard.'

'I was too busy with the Holy Office, but one thing did puzzle me. Dear John said he has sixteen children. Now how is that possible?'

'All is possible with God,' Milford's eyes sparkled with malice. 'You are quite right, he must have about fifteen; let's see,' he began to count off on his fingers. 'None by his wife—she's a Catholic you know and won't divorce him, but four by Georgie Farr, two of them hooked on 'horse' if I'm not mistaken, then two by—Hilda Walsh, oh, what's the name of that American woman, Simon, the one who designs those vulgar book jackets, is it Walsh?'

'Yes, it's Walsh,' he replied, 'but I think they managed to knock out three between them, though John always denies the paternity of the third, not that it makes a scrap of difference. He never pays any alimony.'

'Exactly, now that's only seven. Three by Antigone Larkin, two by Natalie Anther, two by Lucia Thwaite and this is his second by the current victim. That makes the score. Mind you I don't think Gwendolene is going to be a victim. John is beginning to realise he's over fifty and is becoming quite domestic.'

The Chaplain looked sadly disillusioned. Stella and Simon moved over to the wives of a brace of Irish poets who had little concern for conversation, only for a good look round and the absorption of as much beer and whisky as possible, while the supply lasted.

But there was a muffled roar coming from the lavatory on the lower storey. Apparently it was impossible to gain access.

'Simon,' Miles Milford was white and trembling, 'please come and help. I think it's Jimmy; he must have locked himself in the lavatory and passed out.'

They pushed through the noisy crowd that jammed the staircase.

'Bust it open, Simon, I'm not very good at this sort of thing.'

Armstrong kicked open the door and like a shocked

animal the party jerked into silence. One end of a laundry cord had been tied to the stanchion of the lavatory tank. From the other hung the body of Jimmy Lawrence, dead and slowly revolving.

17

SIMON drank some whisky. It was after two o'clock and if his mind had not been partially dissolved in alcohol, he would have realised with some repulsion that he felt more satisfaction at Jimmy Lawrence's death than grief. It let him out of it. He was not responsible for Laura's death. He was not someone who, like Miles, contributed to the destruction of other people. He had suffered from the delusions of an infected mind and made people suffer, but with the aid of others who loved him, as well as his own intelligence and work, he had done something to enlighten and exorcise his feelings. He did not think of the last words of his *Cult of the Vampire*, 'No one is safe unless he realises continually that he can never be in a state of safety.' Nor did he realise that the vindictive powers he was involved with had been conjured up, and with deadly concern, by the image and death smell of Jimmy Lawrence's hanging body; that they were pressing into the rift of his alcoholic euphoria with an intensity which could not be stemmed by his sodden mind.

'Jimmy's death was a kind of ritual. It has relieved me of the guilt of potential murder;' he did not realise that the thought was not his own and would have shocked his waking mind by its callous inanity.

'I feel terrible about that poor boy,' said Stella, 'If only I'd followed my instinct and tried to talk to him. He would talk to me, you know. In fact he told me he was going out with a girl and trying to break with Miles and get a job. I was too late.'

'Ah well,' said Simon, pouring himself another whisky, 'no use crying over spilt milk.'

'Christ's sake, what are you talking about? It's not milk that's been spilt, it's a man's blood.'

The power that was using his tongue realised it had not been tactful and had failed to correspond to a morality which it did not share but which was current in the world, on which it was a parasite.

'Of course, you're right; I'm too tired to register. Despite Milford's admirable novels, the man's like an octopus with his boy friends. That's three to his credit.'

'And what the hell do you mean by that "credit". You make it sound like a Yankee soldier notching up redskins. The boy's dead. He was going out with that girl, Monica Beckett, trying to make a different life, but she'd chucked him over because he refused to leave Milford, or rather hadn't the money to get shot of him.'

'He had neither the will nor the money. But let's not talk about him till tomorrow. What with finishing the book and the party, I'm all in. I'll take a sleeping tablet and go to bed.'

'Not sodium amytol.'

'I think there are three or four left; do you want one?'

'I certainly don't. Remember Charles said you must keep off barbiturates. They lay you open to violence. Don't you realise? Please don't take any...'

'All right, love, just to please you. But I am quite sure *The Cult of the Vampire* has exorcised my demons.'

Professor Armstrong walked unsteadily to the bathroom and clicked the latch. He sluiced his face in cold water and then, the creature of a destructive energy which had completely usurped his own will, took out a bottle from the medicine cupboard and swallowed three blue capsules.

As Simon woke crying out of sleep, he saw for a moment the crouched body of an animal in the open doorway. He moistened his lips and they tasted salt on his tongue. He licked his fingers, they were salt and sticky.

'Oh my God!' He turned on the light and felt as if the point of a stake was driving into his heart. The pillow was red and sopping with blood. This must be another nightmare. He bit on his lip but this time there was no awaking. His hands were scratched and crusted with blood. His wife's head lay on the pillow, her eyes bruised and closed, her lips cut, her nose blood-choked and crooked. She did not move. He did not think she was breathing.

145

'It is not possible to continue.' He groped to the kitchen, and turned on the gas poker. He turned it off again. 'Suicide is not the way out. It will make it even worse for them. There must be another way of paying my debts.' He heard Stella moaning. 'Thank God she is still alive.'

'Why,' she moaned, 'why, why, why.'

He went to the bathroom, carefully moistened a sponge in warm water, took a soft towel and smoothed the dried blood from his wife's mouth and nostrils.

'Why,' she moaned, 'why, why, why?'

'I don't know; I did this; some . . . creature did it through me, used me. I feel that I saw it at the door. Stella, where can I go from here? I know now that it may always happen again. That I am possessed. I cannot think of any way out. I do love you more than my life, but it seems that I . . . that It wishes to kill you. What can I do?'

'My head aches so much and my throat hurts. Is it bleeding?'

Simon felt as if the stake was twisting further into his heart. There were bruises and tooth marks near her jugular vein, one centimetre nearer and she would have been dead.

'I can't say anything,' Stella sobbed, 'I can't help you any more; give me one of those pills, I want to sleep.'

Simon walked back to the bathroom, opened the medicine cupboard and took out the bottle. It was empty. So that was the immediate precipitant of this horror. It seemed that ghosts could use chemistry.

'It appears I have taken them.'

She half raised herself on one bruised elbow and looked at him. 'But you promised.'

'I know, but it seems something else does not keep promises . . . has a different intention.'

'Give me some brandy then.'

He poured out half a tumbler and helped his wife up from the pillow, feeling her body shrink unwillingly from his killing hands. She gulped down the spirits still sobbing, 'You promised, you promised.'

'I was not aware that I took them. I have become a puppet.'

'I cannot help you any more, then. No more, no more.'

146

Simon saw the keys of his car on the mantelpiece. He put on his clothes and then walked towards the telephone in the front room. 'Please God he'll be at home.'

Someone lifted the receiver: 'Abbott here.'

'Charles, it's me, Simon, please, for God's sake, come over to the house now.'

His friend sighed deeply over the phone. 'Of course, Simon, if it's really necessary. Can't you brief me?'

'I can't now. But please come and you will understand. The beast has won. Please come and look after Stella and Rhoda. Stella may have to go to hospital.'

'Immediately,' there was acute anxiety in his friend's voice. 'What about you?'

'I will take care of myself. I shan't be here when you come but I'll leave the key in the latch. Goodbye, Charles, thank you.'

He put the receiver down and touched his wife's moist cheek.

'Goodbye, Simon,' she murmured, 'Goodbye.'

Professor Armstrong knew what to do. He went into the brilliant starry night, opened the garage door, then backing out into the quiet street, started to drive towards the Welsh cottage he had not visited since Laura's death.

18

ABBOTT let himself into the house and very quietly walked upstairs, dreading what he knew he might see in the Armstrongs' bedroom.

'No, this is not what I had expected, this is too much.'

The dressing table mirror was smashed and fragments of glass shone over hairbrushes and Stella's innumerable bottles of scent. One of the chairs lay crushed on the floor as if it had been stamped on, the door which led into the dressing room hung loose on its hinges, the lock broken from its holding, lying on the carpet among splinters of wood. One curtain had been wrenched from the window and sagged from the broken pelmet.

Slow and terrified, he turned towards the bed and noticed the mess of blood on the pillow and outer sheet. But Stella was alive, thank God, lying face downwards, her body twitching violently under the torn soiled coverlets. He walked towards her. 'Stella'—for a moment she stopped shaking, then her face thrust down into the pillows and she began to scream, 'No, no, no, no.'

He bent over her. 'It's me, love, it's Charles, it's Charles, Charles Abbott.'

Slowly the words came through to her and she turned towards him. He noticed the teeth marks on her throat, the swollen, torn mouth, the half-closed left eye and with further shock that her straight nose had been broken and twisted sideways.

'Charles, it's you! Christ! Charles,' she was in his arms, sobbing. He held her to him.

'No, don't let him, don't let it come near me again, ever, ever, ever.'

'I won't darling, really I won't, you're safe now.'

'You promise?'

'Yes, I promise.'

Slowly the sobs quietened and he turned over the pillow and laid her back gently. 'I'm going to get you something to drink and make you more comfortable, I shan't be a moment.'

'Oh Charles...'

'Don't talk now.'

'You won't leave me.'

'I promise I won't, I shall stay now and I'll take you and Rhoda to my flat tomorrow.'

Stella relaxed and stopped trembling. He put on the kettle, got some surgical spirit, cotton wool and plaster from the medicine cupboard, his hands shaking. He had known homicidal violence before, but this concerned two people he loved dearly and had isolated Simon from him with the finality of death.

'At least I can be calm.' His hands were cool and deft again as he swabbed Stella's throat and neck with the spirit and placed a piece of plaster over her torn throat. 'You mustn't blow your nose, breathe through your mouth; try not to blow it.'

'Will I be all right again?'

'Of course you will, it's only for a few hours.'

He gave her a cup of hot sweet tea mixed with a sedative, trying to keep his own cup from trembling and to help her deal with the enormity of an event which had shattered a form of life like an explosive.

'A party, Miles, that boy, suicide,' she jerked out the words, knowing what they must lead to.

'Go on darling, you must tell me.'

'When we came home, Simon didn't seem to respond to it properly, the awfulness of that boy's death. He drank a tumbler of neat whisky and seemed almost pleased about it, the boy's death I mean, as if it was a relief to him; then there were some capsules of sodium amytol left—he must have taken them.'

'I'd warned him against that stuff; they're fatal for him, particularly with drink.'

'I woke up about two o'clock and he wasn't beside me. There was the sound of bumping about in the next room and a kind of muttering and grumbling; he was knocking into the furniture. I thought he was drunk and had gone to get some water but couldn't find the switch, so I called

"Are you all right, Simon?"

' "Simon, Simon?" It wasn't his voice at all and there was the sound of chuckling, someone else from a different part of the room. I was suddenly terrified and leapt up and locked the door . . . Oh God!'

Abbott reached out and took Stella's hand. 'You must go on, but I'm with you now, and you're safe. I won't let anything hurt you.'

'The door handle turned and someone pushed against the door. When whatever it was—for it wasn't Simon, it wasn't—couldn't get in there was a growling noise and, yes, it scratched on the wood; I could hear the nails scraping, then it began to growl, louder and louder, a sort of gasping. I was terrified and got out of bed to escape, to run into the street, to go to the neighbours. But there was a crash and the door fell open. I can't describe . . .'

'You must try.'

'It wasn't Simon, I'm sure of that. I couldn't even recognise the pyjamas; he, it had taken them off and was naked. It stood in the door, its eyes half closed and blinking, turning away from the electric light as if it was painful. Its body was crouched forward and the arms seemed abnormal, long, they almost touched the floor, like an animal that found it difficult to walk upright. Its head was thrust forward too and bunched over a lump of moving muscle. The nose was different. I mean the sides of the nostrils were curved back and left holes in the face, black holes that were snuffing for me because it couldn't see properly. "Simon," I screamed, "wake up . . . Simon."

'It loped across the room and got hold of me by the throat. And then, then it must have slammed me in the face because I pitched forward through flashing lights into blackness. When I came round, I could feel blood trickling from my nose. "Darling," I said, "Look what you've done to me, you must wake up." The creature that had taken my husband's body crouched down over me and believe me, Charles, I'm not being hysterical, this is true; its breath didn't smell of drink, but meat, rotten meat.

' "Darling?" I can't describe the voice but it wasn't drink, it seemed just to find speech difficult and it seemed not only to come from its black lips—they were black and wrinkled—but from all over the room, perhaps because I was half stunned. "But darling," the voice, or rather the voices muttered. "Darling's gone and we're here and there're many of us. If you want Simon Armstrong he isn't here to help you. Man's gone and it's us now, us, us, us."

'I tried to say the rite of exorcism, "In nomine Patris, et Filii." "No," it ripped my collar open, and bit downwards my throat, growling. I didn't feel anything, I was too numbed with fear, but it hurts now, Charles, it really does.'

'I'll give you something for it in a few minutes, but go on now.'

'What I can't make out is where Simon had gone and how the voice seemed to come from all over the room.

' "You don't put us off with words any more, because we're too strong for you, too strong for S—Simon Armstrong, that man, too strong for Ch—Charles Abbott, too strong for any man. Too strong. We are many. Us, us." That last word,' Stella whispered, 'it seemed to grow and grow until it filled the whole room, until it seemed to be a part of it. Then I blacked out again.'

'A good thing,' said Abbott, 'if you were unconscious through pain and shock; I mean then you could have made a barrier and stopped whatever happened in this room getting at you.'

'I woke up again. It was Simon bending over me. He looked terrified, confounded, he remembered nothing, but I can't go back to him, I can't, I can't. It's too frightening.'

'You shall not. I will see to it.' Abbott got to his feet, walked unsteadily towards the kitchen, made some more tea and adding a lot of sugar and another sedative to one of the cups brought it to Stella, feeling a sense of loss as if his many years of friendship with Armstrong had been more finally disrupted than by his death from a cliff fall or a skidding car. 'Us, us,' and whatever his friend's present state of mind, he was still the creature of that intolerable matrix of subhuman hatred.

'Drink this, love, it will take the pain away, and I'll sit up now and smoke a bit, it's almost morning. Then to-morrow you and Rhoda must come to my flat. Sleep now.'

Stella drank her laced tea, and leaned back into sleep, her mouth open, breathing heavily, but, Abbott noticed, with a reassuring regularity. She would get over this.

He lit a cigar and leaned back in an arm-chair as the first light glinted through the torn curtain and birds began to stir and twitter in the garden.

This vicarious life he had chosen to live through other people. Its pains and necessity. But what about Stella and Rhoda now, what would he do if Simon returned? All his professional knowledge affirmed the danger and impossibility of such a reunion. But Simon was completely dissociated from what had happened and what had possessed him. He might attempt it. He looked at the bruised and ravaged face of Stella and realised that whatever happened, whatever pleas were made he could not allow his friend to meet her again. The milkman's bottles clinked in the porch. It was seven o'clock. Stella, Rhoda ... Simon, in whom centred this nightmare of the battered face, the broken mirror, the lock which lay in splinters upon the carpet, they did not dissolve in the thin good light of a new morning. He who had previously been the detached ironic interpreter of life was now its creature. The fact of Stella and Rhoda, the women who were coming to his flat for protection from a by no means intangible danger, this fact with its intricacies of indecision took him wholly to itself. And what of Armstrong? The climbing, the talk, the infinite varieties of good humour and misunderstanding, were only vapour. The obsession had won and the man he had known seemed dissipated by the ravaged bedroom he sat in. It had always been a losing battle against powers which might, in the end, be subject to his engrossing curiosity, but at the moment seemed too terrible to be a theme of speculation. But Simon would return, the wish for life was strong in him, for love, for relationship. He could not allow this to happen again, not to Stella, to Rhoda, to any living being. The dead were in charge of the man now. What was it, obsession? But the physical changes and this complete and unadulterated violence; he thought of the extraordinary plasticity of flesh and spirit under such compulsion. But the voices from all over this broken room and—he believed

Stella—the elongated arms, the bared nostrils! Dr Abbott gazed into an unlimited darkness beyond either his personal or professional understanding and, gazing, knew that whatever happened, upon him lay the responsibility of caring for Stella and her adopted daughter. Eight o'clock, the door bell rang and he opened the door to collect his friend's post. He glanced down at the large package—Naughton and James; it must be the proofs of *The Cult of the Vampire*.

The M1, then the A5, Wellington, Shrewsbury, Llangollen. Simon drove fast but with extreme care, partly because he did not wish to inflict any further injury, partly because he wished to identify with a machine, become a clutch, a steering wheel, a gear lever, to be a thing, to feel nothing. But the horror of the night sluiced back irresistibly. He had played a game with his Destiny, and lost. Understanding had not been enough. He had tried, like the charioteer of the Upanishads, to merge the two horses, one bent on lucidity, the other on chaos, but the dark horse of Kali had taken over and never again could he control it, be safe, or offer to those he loved either love or safety. He drove his car through Corwen towards the loud hills of Wales. 'If I went back again for rapport, regained Stella's love and confidence, it still would not be safe.' He looked at his own hands—those grippers and killers.

He turned left from the A5 into the long sinuous road that led past the village and the Lake of Bala. Now he was coasting alongside the blue streak of the lake that he had passed so many times with Laura; he had wished to believe that he himself shared the controlled tranquillity of the landscape, when all the time this nemesis had been waiting for him on the edge of all things. Mist fumed over the morning waters. The cold, stripped, indifferent granite hovered over the roadside but cast no shadow. There was no escape. Two, three, four years then the charioteer would doze off again; the reins unloosed, the bat-winged creature would plunge down and away. The next attack would be final.

He drove up from the crinkled metal of Lake Bala, away from human love, striving to be mechanical, to be no one. Now he was coasting downwards to Blaenau and tried not to remember how Laura and he, after the long grind from London, had always stopped at the village pub for a glass of beer.

'Lord, let this cup pass from me.'

Now he could see the enormous vague outlines of Cnicht and the Moelwyns plunging down like ships towards him through streamers of mist. Sheep lay for warmth on either side of the thin road. At last he realised with complete finality that the phenomena he loved existed no more. That he himself, the mountains, the bright rain-rinsed world had dwindled to the single pin-pointed fact of potential murder.

He slowed down for the arched right turn into the long winding mountain road that led up to Croesor and then to his cottage. It was a bad road to meet cars on, but it was only five a.m., too early even for farmers, so he could both watch the road and the white lace of falling water that festooned the fellside, the glistening wool mist of the valley, that Laura had so often recorded in her water-colours.

He stopped his car some fifty yards from his cottage. Olwen Roberts was his next-door neighbour, and although he was fond of this woman who had brought up, unaided and well, some six children, who would undoubtedly come down to greet him if she heard his car, he felt any human contact would be like fingers pressing on scorched flesh.

Collies had scratched up the daffodils and snowdrops that Laura had planted and when he opened the door the front room breathed out damp mist.

He found a shilling for the electric meter, made himself some coffee and swallowed the contents of an ancient tin of bully beef. There was an old anorak hanging in the cupboard, the relic of some student to whom he had loaned the cottage. He struggled into it and put on a pair of boots nailed with tricounis. These he would allow himself but he did not take ropes, ice-axe or any slings and karabiners, they were not part of the chance which he felt had been offered to him . . .

'My dearest love,' shivering slightly, Simon sat down at

the kitchen table and wrote to Stella, 'I do not intend to kill myself, but I feel impelled to put my life in the balance and find out by consulting an unusual oracle, that of Llwedd, whether I am intended to live and can even now foster life, or can live and cherish life no longer. I am not taking any rope or axe. This way I may find out what is intended. I think the chances are an even fifty-fifty and I wish whatever is signified by a mountain to decide whether I am to live or die. Please rely on Charles to help you both, and give him my love. I know he will both help and understand. Dear, dear love, forgive me; whether from here or there, my love is with you always.' He pinned the note to the kitchen table, opened the door and left it open so that Olwen would discover its whereabouts, then very quietly walked to his car and drove up to Pen-y-Pass and the mountain of Llwedd.

He arrived there before eight a.m. The carpark attendant was not there, but he placed a pound in an envelope, scribbled 'For Glyn Owen with affectionate wishes, Simon the Poet,' and wedged it behind a windscreen wiper. Then without rope, ice-axe, pitons or other aids he set out for the Ridge Route of Llwedd.

The cat ice crackled under his nailed boots and when he saw the twin peaks of Llwedd in the first sunlight he realised there was more snow on the mountains than he had expected. Long streaks of it covered the grass bands of the West Peak and when he had toiled up the scree to the long easy glacis that started the Ridge, he saw that it was coated with loose powder and verglas and wished for his ice-axe and crampons. Then he thought of Stella lying wounded on her damp pillow, her twisted nose and gashed throat and realised that the question of his temporal survival must be decided by an authority other than his own, that whether or not he was to continue to live must be determined by the mountain. His vibram soles were interspersed at their edges by sharp claw-like tricouni nails as a concession to safety, an equal balancing of the dice, and they held on the snow-coated verglas when he kicked them inwards. The horror forgotten in the complete absorption of climbing, he balanced delicately up the glacis, avoiding wherever possible the great streams of black ice that poured down its shallow gullies. He came to the short terminal wall. It was too steep for ice or snow, and attending to the exact positioning of each footstep he was soon up and over this minor obstacle. There was thick powder snow on the narrow platform above it and looking down to the small plate of rock to the left of the upward slanting groove he saw that it was covered with a slippery mat of ice. He stepped down and looked with complete indifference at the three-hundred feet of sheer cliff-fall that plunged from his footplate. There was no second man behind him safeguarding his next move and, smelling once more even in the tingling chilly air the intolerable blood smell of that soaked pillow, he was glad of his precarious solitude. To live or die—it was no longer his concern.

The steep groove that led upwards to the right and the knife-edge of an arête was choked with hard ice. With an axe there would have been no problem. Simon saw a thin sharp sliver of rock and with an innate sense of self-preservation prised it out of its loose niche in the left wall. Holding on to the niche with his left hand, he bent forward and chipped out a first foothold in the groove, swung his right foot forward and straddled the gap. There was a good left handhold on the far wall. His gloved hand gripped there and with his right he gained purchase and step after step balanced up the groove, realising just how great was the margin of safety he had allowed himself on previous climbs. He was up on the arête now with its firm holds, and moving steadily towards the crux of the Ridge Route. The platform at the foot of the wall, from whose twin cracks Charles had once moved a kitchen poker, was coated with ice now. Simon punched a take-off place into it with his rock spike. Two ravens honked and swirled above his head, looping in the slight wind that spattered his face with particles of snow. Laura had loved the spring acrobatics of these dark birds, their delight in themselves and the element that sustained them. Laura, Stella. The twin cracks above him were heavily iced. If he used his spike he could chip holds into them and the pitch would be feasible. Again he saw the blood-stained crooked nose of Stella and heard her reiterated question, 'Why, why, why?'

Simon raised his hand and flung the stone from him; some seconds later he heard it tinkle on the scree six-hundred feet below. It was necessary for the mountain to decide. He turned, and with no sense of fear, only of a problem to be solved, looked at the wall. The twin central peaks were levelled out with ice and unclimbable. But the wall was in reality a wide groove and it might be possible to use its enclosing side walls. He raised his left boot and with one hand pressed against the right wall, strained upwards to gain a small foothold some four feet above him. It reached and held there. Very slowly he worked further upwards with his cupped right hand, pushed his fingers into a small side crack and jammed them shut. That gave him some purchase for a further move. He levered his right foot upwards and kicked into an ice-choked crack. The spiked tricouni points bit and held there. He knew that where the poker had been jammed there must be a large ice-free spike for his left hand some four feet above him; reach that and the problem would be over. He worked his left hand slowly upwards and felt the rounded base of the spike. Four more inches at most and he would have grasped it.

His tricouni points slipped from the icehold. Blindly he clawed for the kitchen poker his friend had removed, slithered downwards, and gathering speed, bounced on and away from the ice patch at the foot of the groove, plummeting out from the mountain face, out and down to the footrocks. The seconds were extended; passing the innumerable man-travelled grooves and terraces of the mountain, he spun through his own most intricate life. His mother and father rejecting the gift of being human, the good gift they had been offered, John Chester swaying towards him on bruised thighs, Daphne sobbing and lolling over her slopped table, Flora MacGrotty, the beast in the doorway, the beast that was himself, all the twittering fauna of nightmare thinned behind him as he plunged. He knew now. All the perversions, the tortuous exploitation, the infinite varieties of cruelty asserted, even by their unremitting denial, whatever could be signified by that word 'love' which, as he span outwards and downwards, he could at long last utter with complete conviction. The faces of Laura and Stella rose to meet him. They would have been one and two people if personality was valid here. But it's quite different now, thought Simon Armstrong, as his body exploded upon the sharp footrocks of Llwedd.